Black Fin
An Orca's Journey
G. Jeffrey Ares

Book Cover by Eric Swartz

Illustration by Ethan Gent

First edition 2024

TABLE OF CONTENTS

Dedicated to the wolves of the sea

Chapter One
THE NEWBORN

Her name is Herynn, and this would be her third calf. She swam escorted by two male orcas. The female orca's companions weighed in at eleven and nine thousand pounds each and are her offspring from six and three seasons past. Herynn had named the oldest Joop and his brother Joom. They are both devoted to their mother always.

Herynn is the matriarch of her pod. She keeps all her offspring close to her, but eventually the males will leave the pod. Her two sons swim in a close circle around her. They provide comfort and protection. It was time.

The three orcas enter a shallow cove just as the sun was setting. It was a very still night, no breeze. Herynn knew in a few hours' other mothers would be bringing newborns back to the pod as well.

The cold waters of the North Pacific, teeming with life, would be their home. She would be a mother again. In a couple of hours, she would return to the pod to introduce her newborn. All that matters to Herynn is her families survival.

The pain in her abdomen comes in pulses, and her swimming slows. Herynn hovered a few feet below the surface. Her contractions increased. It would be soon. She just knew.

In the shallows of the cove, the little one emerged. The tail first, followed by a black body with a peachy white belly. Then the pectoral fins folded in, and the dorsal fin folded down; collagen would later stretch it into position to help the newborn swim level. Next, a perfect black head, with white slashes behind its new eyes. A mouth already filled with teeth and lungs eager to breathe

the ocean air. All this happened in under a minute.

There is blood in the water from the birth, and the two smaller orcas taste this and become more cautious. Joop and Joom are both on high alert as they patrol the area around Herynn.

Mother sees and feels her new calve, but he is a bit smaller than normal. She brings him to the surface for his first breath of air. The newborn inhales, and puffs air and mist back out a very tiny blowhole. Now his life in the sea is ready to begin.

The air is cool and fresh, and soon the night sky over Alaska will be filled with stars. The light of the moon reflects off the water's surface. She clicks and chirps to her newborn, she coos to him and nuzzles his body. She needs to name him and thinks for a moment. She decides on Okent.

Then the female orca clicked and chirped to her newborn, "I am your mother, I am called Herynn." She pauses, then clicks, "your name is Okent."

Mother and baby are only together for a couple of hours when her guards are alerted to the presence of danger. She hears their squeal of danger.

There is a warning from the males; urgent clicks, and chirps. Herynn knows immediately to protect her son. She rushes to hide the newborn. Herynn leads him to an even more shallow area, full of sea kelp and underwater rocks. The female orca clicks and chirps to her newborn. "Please stay here until I return, please Okent, listen to mother." She nuzzles her newborn for a few precious moments, then darts away.

The two male orcas are searching for the threat using their echolocation abilities. All their senses are on high alert. Something is approaching them.

Two great white sharks each measuring a length of eighteen feet had moved into the area, having picked up the scent of a recent birth. Their nostrils picked up the tiniest molecules of blood and they begin tracking its source.. Hundreds of tiny openings cover the undersides of each shark's snout. These openings allow them to smell prey and taste the water. Each shark has a sensory array that runs down their sides from gills to tail, called the Ampullae of Lorenzini. This organ enables the shark to feel electrical impulses in the water.

The sharks sensed there were four heartbeats in the water ahead. They increased their pace, each darting left and right to lock in on their prey.

The two young adult male orcas swim in a distraction pattern to keep the threat away from mother and baby. Herynn clicked, whistled, and used head movements to direct her escorts. Joop and Joom followed every command immediately. This gave Herynn a few precious moments to hide Okent.

The sharks were almost in a frenzy, sensing so much movement in the water and seeing flashes of black and white. Mouths full of a never-ending supply of teeth, gnashing at the extremely fast and agile orcas. Twisting and bending, trying to bite the young males. Then it happened, one of the male orcas moved wrong, it swam and turned too aggressively past the shark and could not correct its course fast enough.

The shark bit down on Joop's tail, leaving a crescent-shape bite on the orca's fluke. The orca felt pain and cried out a high-pitched squeal, whining and clicking to his brother. But the second orca was too busy trying to stay away from its own attacking shark to help.

Herynn was aware of everything happening in front of her. She used this distraction to flank the sharks. Her brain was the second heaviest of all ocean water mammals and her intelligence was keen and sharp. She was a perfect apex predator with no fear of the attackers. Her only thought was to protect Okent. The newborn was just under six hours old, and already experiencing the dangers of the sea. Herynn made the young males aware of her intentions using chirps, clicks, and whistles.

Now, the female orca began her own attack.

She gathered tremendous speed, her flukes pumping up and down with incredible power. She brought her twelve-thousand-pound body to full speed and crashed into the first shark's left side, crushing all the internal organs and killing the brute immediately. The gray and white threat twitched in an underwater death dance. The two male orcas swooped in to tear the great fish apart. The shark's liver became a quick snack and a burst of energy. The tiny left-over pieces that floated away became a meal for any fish or crab on the bottom.

Herynn's second attack was just as vicious, defending her newborn and her pod family with cunning and force. No threat would ever stop her. She swooped around like a jet fighter banking. The second shark had moved out of the two male orcas view. The shark was using the death of its brother to divert the orcas and to find its young prey.

Herynn knew that the second shark was searching for her newborn. Her speed increased and she rushed toward the Okent's hiding place. The threat was suddenly ahead of her. Herynn recognized the beast to be a killer of orca young ones. Herynn determined that the shark's length was less than her twenty-eight, which was good for the female orca. The matriarch knew exactly what to do.

She dove below the great white shark and came up under its torso. Hitting the threat with all her might, she tore the shark's belly open using the momentum of her six tons traveling at just over thirty knots. Her teeth ripped at its insides, slashing and shaking the internal organs. Blood and sinew floated everywhere around the shark.

The beast twisted and shuddered; its life was over. No more threat. She circled the body as it drifted toward the bottom. Herynn thoughts were *It is Dead... Killed... Defeated*
And then...

Okent had stayed where his mother put him, floating amongst the seaweed and kelp. He was too new to the ocean world to really understand all of Herynn's words. *"You must wait here, Okent, stay here, stay hidden."*

Okent was becoming afraid. He started to feel little bumps and touches on his sides. He saw flashes of movement and motion. Then suddenly a pair of brown eyes were staring at him.

Okent blinked and then the eyes were gone. Another pair of eyes appeared, and then disappeared just as quickly. Okent realized these were the eyes of a different creature.

They bumped into him but swam away so quickly, he could hardly make them out. They had smooth bodies and strong agile front flippers, and were making bubbles and poking him. During a pause of their torment, Okent took a chance and darted away from the seals. He bolted to the open water of the cove and quickly became confused. Panic set in as he could not find any safe area. He was lost and confused. He clicked and chirped and cried out for his mother. He swam about making half circles, clicking for Herynn all the while. Okent chirped and called out again, and again asking for help, but no one came.

The newborn orca floated near the surface, barely breathing and unwilling to move. Okent sensed the ocean around him and became aware of the great openness. The newborn orca was terrified and decided to swim back the way he came but became disoriented and lost. He started to feel an emptiness in his stomach, and his thoughts were, *I am alone.* Okent needed to find his mother for protection and to feed. He chirped and clicked again and again, but still there was no answer. "Mother? I am here! Mother?"

The ocean tide began moving the little orca further away from his previous hiding area.

Okent cried out in long squeals. "I am lost mother!" "Help me."

Chapter Two
LOST

"**O** kent?!"

Herynn could not find her newborn, "No!" she cried "Where are you? She thought, *why did you move from the safety of the kelp?*" She swam in confused zig zag directions with great speed calling for him. Searching, swimming, calling, over and over.

"Where are you Okent?"

She felt her own heart break, she did not want to surface for air, the loss was unbearable.

"Where has he gone? was he taken? Okent?"

Herynn let out long crying screams for minutes at a time piercing the ocean.

Her young male companions found her floating on top of the water near the area where she left Okent. She chirped to Joop and Joom, "Look for him NOW!" Both orcas darted away and began a circular search pattern. They looked for hours. The presence of seals and sting rays were everywhere, which was very distracting to the orcas. It prevented Okent from being echolocated.

Joop and Joom returned to Herynn. They were quiet and said nothing. She knew it was time to return to the safety of the Pod. Joop was in pain from the shark bite. He was losing a small amount of blood, but the flow was slowing down. Joop would be okay in the safety of the pod and would have a scar to show off to the other young males. Together they escorted Herynn back to the others. The female orca paused every few hundred yards and echolocates the area. She senses nothing, except a faint echo of seals.

Joom and Joop will tell the pod of Herynn's bravery. How she alone killed the threat. Then they will tell the pod about the loss of Okent.

CHAPTER THREE
BABEL

A great whale was submerged just below the surface of the ocean, not too far from shore. The early morning sun had just begun to warm the air. She had just given birth to her fourth calf. This calf had arrived two months earlier than the typical eleven months of gestation. Calves are born just before the southern migration begins.

The baby was unresponsive. Babel had pushed it to the surface but the calf would not take a breath; the whale was still born. This was the second calf she had lost. Babel had waited three long years between births, and she had refused the advances of several bulls while mourning the loss of her third calf.

Babel had traveled to the breeding grounds off the shores of Hawaii, accepted a male of her choosing, and then she began her year long journey back to the coast of Mexico and then on to Alaskan waters to give birth.

Now it had happened again, and her soul was crushed. She watched as her newborn floated away. Babel drifted for hours, barely breathing, not wanting to live. She knew this might have been her last chance at raising a newborn as her breeding days were growing much shorter. She floated toward shore to a cluster of coves with shallow water all filled with kelp. She could hear seals swimming around her, and they were not afraid of her, but they never came close. There was a respect for her size and strength. Babel felt that the seals were trying to get her attention, but she chose to ignore them. She just wanted to be alone. In the distance Babel heard crying, and a call for help. She did not concern herself with this as the clicks were unfamiliar and Babel continued to weep.

The late morning had arrived, and the day was beginning to warm up. There was a slight breeze blowing. Babel floated with the tide current, bringing her further into the shallows. This could be dangerous, as her size could strand her on the shore, so she corrected her path. Still floating, Babel started singing of her loss to the other humpbacks in her pod, several miles northwest of her. The adults, teenagers, and newborns all would weep with her. Babel told the pod not to wait for her, she needed time to mourn.

Babel was still aware of her environment. All of the life in the ocean around her continued to swim and scurry about. All creatures were dwarfed by her immense size. She knew her calf would sink to the bottom and become food for the many sea creatures down below. She knew this was the way of the ocean, and the final resting place of all humpback whales.

The tide changed and she found herself parallel to the shore. There were many rocks, caves and an abundance of seaweed and kelp.

This would have been a perfect place for a newborn to rest after its birth.

Suddenly Babel sensed a small presence approaching her. Something gentle and infantile. She heard a small voice that was asking for help. She felt a caress, and then there was a gentle tug on her teat, an excited mouth was drinking her milk. The smallest heart beating pulse was detected by the great whale. She clicked quietly, "My baby?"

She rolled on her side to allow this hungry mouth better access to her milk. She embraced the joy of a young life feeding from her. Babel's mind filled with questions; *are you my baby? Have you come back to me?*

She thought, *this little creature does not feel like my newborn. What was this tiny being? Who was this creature? It has no fear of my size.*

Babel had to see, so she moved her great head for a better view of the creature. But her eyes were only a source of shadows and light and some vision. Humpbacks are monochromatic, so they cannot see colors like red and green. Her eyes gave her a dark and light mass with movement. Her sense of touch gave her the rest. Babel knew right away that this creature was different than her own kind. She also knew that the small dark shaded being, no bigger than half the length of her pectoral fin, was scared and hungry.

This newborn was not gray skinned; it was not beautiful like her other surviving calves and it had a very different shape. She realized this creature's skin colors were black and white, this was when Babel recognized it as a natural predator to all her kind.

How lost and frightened it must have been to approach her. This small being was asking for help that only she could give. The matriarch humpback thought to herself, *nurse as much as you need to my water child.* She covered the little stranger with one of her huge pectoral fins.

After a long while, the newborn had finished nursing and floated in place. Babel asked, "What is your name? How have you come to me?"

The orca answered, the best he could using clicks and chirps. He had very little memory of the previous night, memories of hiding in kelp and seeing big brown eyes staring at him. Okent clicked, "They poked me." He chirped and clicked again, "I was very frightened and very hungry, I had to swim away."

Babel explained to the newborn orca, that those eyes he saw were seals. "They are not threats to you or me, but now little one you should rest."

After a few more hours passed and Okent bobbed up and down very close to his new protector. He tried to breathe in unison with Babel and puffs of mist laden air would shoot from each of their blowholes. Okent had to take six breaths for every one of Babel's. Pfft! Pfft! Pfft! Pfft! Pfft! POOF! Babel's breathing was much louder than that of a newborn. Okent felt comfort in the sound of her breathing as they swam together bonding, touching and learning each other's sea life rhythms.

A whole day and night had passed. In the early morning, Babel realized she could not leave the newborn. He would not survive on his own, so she made the decision right then to make this baby orca her own.

Babel would tell the pod of her return with a song. She had something special to show the other humpbacks. Babel ushered Okent forward with her enormous pectoral fin and they began to swim northwest. The pod was more than fifteen miles away by now. She thought, *I have lost a newborn and found a newborn.* She began to sing, "Thank you, my creator."

The female humpback never considered the reaction of the pod to Okent. She is Babel, and she is one of the elders. The pod will respect her decision.

During the journey northwest Babel remembered the stories her elders told of the creator. It was known that the creator was from the stars and would return to the humpback pods. Many, many seasons would pass, and then there would be a great gathering of humpbacks. They all just knew where to meet and wait. Thousands and thousands of humpback whales would look to the stars and hear a wonderful voice in their thoughts. Each whale would hear a song asking them, "How do you fare? Do you like the ocean I have given you all?" There would be many, many responses from the humpbacks and the sea would be filled with clicks and whistles and whale songs. The voice would continue by reminding the whales that were gathered to always enjoy your ocean world and give love to your offspring. The songs were just suddenly in all their thoughts. Then the entire pod would begin what was called "The Floating." Each whale would slowly face nose down, with their tail pointing straight up. It was thought that the creator would do the same and all the pod members would stay like this until the creator wished them goodbye, promising to return. The creator would call to all of them with songs, "Be good to each other."

Each humpback had a vision placed in their thoughts of the creator's enormous size and long cylindrical shape, mostly resembling the body of a humpback whale. On the bottom of the cylindrical object, a strange light would reach down holding a glowing orb. When the visit was over, the creator would move back toward the stars, always promising to return at another time. A chanting could be heard in their minds, *"Be good to each other, be good to each other, be good to each other."*

The humpbacks would decide individually when to begin surfacing so some remained vertical for longer periods of time than others. There was always a great feeling of peace among the pods after this gathering. Babel hoped to experience this event before her time in the ocean came to an end. Her desire to live returned to her as she now had a very small and frightened reason.

CHAPTER FOUR
THE POD

They had all heard the story of Babel's loss by now. They sang sad songs and moved slowly, waiting for Babel to find them. She had communicated with the pod across many miles that she was on her way back and she had found a miracle and wanted to show them. She thought for a moment, then sang, "I am not too old to be a mother."

Babel swam closer to the pod and asked the others not to be afraid. "Please know I have a very small newborn with me." The females in the pod sensed the strangeness first. They immediately gathered close to their young ones. This newborn was not a humpback. The males of the pod began to react and circle the females and the young. Then a very large bull turned and went to greet Babel. The bull was named McKeel. No one knew who gave him that name or if it had a meaning. McKeel feared nothing in the ocean, his size and strength saw to that. The great humpback's length was fifty-nine feet and he weighed thirty-five tons. No one knew McKeel's age, not even McKeel. The great humpback was the patriarch of the pod and was given the utmost respect. He clicked a long low tone to Babel, more curious than anything else. "Who is this newborn with you?"

There was a hesitation from the female humpback which prompted McKeel to click, "Again, I ask, who is this, Babel, and why do you protect him?" "He is not like us; his kind hunts us." "Please tell me why he is with you."

Babel explained as best she could how she came across the newborn after losing her calf. She told McKeel she would adopt him, and he would become her son. Babel clicked, "We will teach him our ways." Then she bellowed very loudly, to show she was serious "I have spoken! Am I clear?" McKeel thought for a moment as he always thought before speaking. The old humpback has always been the wisest in the pod. McKeel knew it was best to not argue with Babel at this time.

He then asked, "what is this newborns name?"

Babel clicked and cooed to Okent. "This is McKeel, tell him your name." The newborn responded to McKeel very quietly, "My name is Okent." McKeel looked the little orca up and down, reserving any judgment.

When McKeel spoke again, he expressed concerned to Babel. He said, "this creature will not be accepted into the pod. He will upset the others and he may someday hurt one of the pod."

Babel explained, "I will teach him about our pod life. I will teach him to live like a humpback. We will all show him love and acceptance, and in time all will understand. There is nothing else to discuss."

McKeel thought it would be best to just let her pass, so he slowly turned toward the pod. He cautiously watched the newborn while they all swam toward the other humpbacks. "Stay behind me," McKeel advised. Babel and Okent slowed to follow the wise bull. Okent watched McKeel's great flukes move ahead of him, barely moving up and down. It was a challenge to keep up with both his new mother and the big whale.

Chapter Five
THE TRIO

The trio moved closer to the pod. When they were a mile away, McKeel paused and spoke "Let me go ahead." McKeel wanted to talk with the other humpbacks alone. The old bull would explain of Babel's decision and what was about to happen. McKeel would clear the way for the mother and newborn to join the humpbacks. He knew the members of the pod would be nervous. Who among them ever heard of such a thing, a humpback caring for a baby orca.

In humpback pods it is common for newborns to be adopted by other nursing whales. Sometimes, a mother humpback passes or becomes ill, and the newborn's care falls to another. Young calves are often looked after by their aunties. This could be an older sister or just another female in the pod.

All newborns are to be protected in the pod and Babel would make sure of this with Okent. Babel and the baby orca approached the pod, maybe sixty yards out now. They both remained there while the pod adjusted to this peculiar situation. Babel knew not all the pod members would be accepting of Okent.

Many mothers moved their newborns away, other whales kept their distance as well. A few large bulls came up close to see the newborn and take in his shape and size. They had no fear of this tiny creature. The bulls clicked and sang to Babel, and issued a warning to keep him in check and away from the young ones. Babel reminded all the bulls of her position in this pod, and respect was to be shown to her and her newborn. Her clicks were loud and carried great authority. Babel understood the bulls' concerns and decided to stay in the rear of the pod. She knew it would take time for the others to adjust, and trust her decision. She would be patient and let time pass, because now, she had a newborn to care for.

Okent sensed all the tension around him, so he stayed very close to his new mom. He stayed even closer to her when the bulls came up to Babel, and he even held his breath so as to not be seen.

Okent was hungry again and wanted to feed. He nuzzled up to Babel, who then rolled slightly to her right exposing the newborn to one of her two nipples, which protrude through her mammary slits. To nurse, the newborn would curl his tongue around the nipple and thick, fatty milk would instantly squirt into the calf's mouth. Soon after, Okent had a very full stomach, and he would slumber next to his mother's right pectoral fin that night. For the first time in several days the baby orca felt he was safe.

The next morning McKeel swam with them, but at a distance. He did his best not to disturb the newborn. He knew his great size would be unnerving to the little creature. He wondered why a fatherly connection was beginning to grow between Okent and himself. McKeel had sired many offspring, as he was the most desired by the female humpbacks in the pod. Still, this little creature had intrigued him like no other, Babel was right in knowing that Okent was special.

The weeks passed and Okent grew. He was nursing more often now, and when Babel needed to rest, he would listen to Mckeel sing. Okent tried to mimic the songs McKeel created, but they never sounded the same.

McKeel would sing to them both throughout the day, and sometimes at night. McKeel knew the best songs to sing, and often created new ones. He was the oldest and wisest of the pod and his songs were about family and survival.

The patriarch was mostly hopeful for Babel and her newborn as he knew she really wanted to keep Okent among the pod. McKeel soon realized that he was spending more and more time with the orca. The great whale thought to himself, *I am beginning to really care for this little black and white hunter of humpbacks.*

Chapter Six
THAT TIME OF YEAR

The time to migrate was approaching. The pod knew it was the season to change their feeding grounds and swim in the great waters. They would travel southwest, using the earth's magnification. Whales can also use celestial navigation and by using the stars they can plot a direction. Large land masses like islands can aid their direction, and even oil rigs.

Humpbacks, like other whales can sing songs that are heard over hundreds of miles away. Whales can be in touch with other pods to always be on a sure course of travel.

The pod would follow the migration routes of their ancestors. The route had been traveled thousands and thousands of times.

They moved as a group for safety and companionship and this is also how a suitable mate is sometimes found.

Babel and Okent would join the pod, but at a rear position. Babel understood this caution, but her position in the pod afforded her great respect from others. She chose to swim in last place with Okent.

Months passed and Okent thrived. The other newborns grew as well. On occasion a newborn would interact with Okent. He enjoyed the short comradery, only to see his new friend be ushered away by an aunty or mother humpback. Okent didn't understand this and asked why.

Babel would do her best to comfort Okent. They had many long conversations and then Babel would ask Okent to be patient. She continued to teach Okent the ways of the humpback. Babel would demonstrate to him how to fish and chase squid. The female humpback would encourage the young orca to copy her to catch food. She would scoop up a great mouthful of water and filter the krill out. Okent had his own way, which was easier for him.

Okent's favorite technique to feed was to submerge below a school of mackerel and blow bubbles and swim in a circle. This would gather the fish in a group. Then the orca would simply rise under them with his mouth open and swallow several fish in one gulp.

Okent still fed on his Babel's milk, though this was becoming less often. He still enjoyed the closeness of his mother and her pectoral fin hugs, always protecting him.

McKeel would make his presence known to Babel and the young orca with songs and clicks. This was a very special time for Okent. McKeel would spend hours with the young orca, teaching him about the ocean. How to navigate the great areas between feeding grounds, and how to defend himself against predators that were big and small. Okent learned the dangers of sharks and the silliness of seals.

The humpbacks greatest lessons were about the surface killers. He taught Okent to avoid the great metal monsters that floated on the surface. The beasts were very dangerous, it was best to stay away, for there is no defense. Okent had many questions about the metal beast. He would ask repeatedly, "Where are they from? Why do they hurt us? Why should we not fight back?" McKeel did his best to answer but he knew Okent was never satisfied with the answers he would give.

Two seasons had passed, and the pod became more accepting of Okent. The young humpbacks and the orca were now allowed to play together. The adults always watched the interaction of their young with Okent with interest. There was a general relief in the pod when the young humpbacks appeared to be growing larger than the orca. All the pod members were expressing some level of comfort with Okent among them.

Babel was a proud mother, and her aunties were helpful with the young orca. The pod flourished and survived the hostilities of the ocean. More newborns arrived and the previous group of newborns were becoming teenagers and young adults. During this time Okent had begun to notice that he was not like the other members of the pod. He was different in size and shape. He was of a different color as well. Okent had questions but chose to keep them to himself for now. He would have to ask McKeel someday about why he was so different.

The young orca knew McKeel would tell him the truth, and this was something he felt he should know, but he also knew that this might be something he did not want to know.

Chapter Seven
BREACHING

Many times, a challenge was issued throughout the pod: Who could leap highest out of the water? All the humpbacks participated, but for different reasons. The older members of the pod would leap and twist in the air only to crash down on their backs. This was done to dislodge parasites and barnacles from their skin. Both creatures were most irritating. Parasites would burrow into their skin causing rashes and itching. Barnacles could grow near sensitive spots on the whale's body, particularly the eyes and blowhole. Then there are remora fish, who would use their built-in sucker on their heads and clamp onto an area near the whale's mouth or underside to catch a free ride. The remora fish were slightly more tolerable because they would feed on a lot of the parasites that the humpbacks had to contend with.

The younger members would of course view the breaching as a sign of becoming an adult. Who would be at the top of the challenge? Who would leap the highest? Okent was no different and he was excited to prove himself.

The young adults, both male and female, would try to outdo each other. One by one they would dive into the depths of the ocean. Humpback after humpback would ascend with great speed, flapping their enormous flukes only to breach the surface and twist in the air. The biggest splashes came from landing on their backs. Great waves were created, and loud thunderous sounds were heard above and below the water surface. The pod would applaud and be delighted at each young humpback's attempt. Clicks and whistles were abundant.

One of the elders asked Babel, "Can your water child breach? He is old enough now, he should try." Babel clicked to her son and asked, "Do you want to try?" Okent chirped a yes without hesitation.

Okent's turn came up and he began his run. He dove down into the dark blue green water and banked upward. He pumped his flukes up and down with all his strength. His speed increased; he was gathering great momentum. Then Okent breached the surface with the slightest splash and leapt into the air. Okent felt like he was going to fly, he was soaring like a seagull. He reached a height of twenty feet before he began to twist his belly skyward.

The orca crashed onto the surface with a great splash. He quickly regained his thoughts and direction. Okent heard many cheers while he looked for Babel. He saw her amongst the adults, and she clicked and whistled how proud she was of her son. Okent thought to himself, *today is a good day, because today I am part of the pod.*

Babel swam to Okent, she rolled and embraced him with a hug. Her enormous flippers wrapped around him. They both floated this way for some time. Then needing a breath, they both surfaced and exhaled a puff of mist each. They both inhaled together, filling their lungs with cool ocean air.

Mother and son would breathe in unison for some time. Okent was feeling safe and welcomed. The humpback pod was his family.

CHAPTER EIGHT
THE SEARCH

Herynn was in deep thought. Having just caught another long distance chirp sound of her newborn, something in the chirps told her Okent was older, and cared for. She knew he was not alone, but the clicking sounds faded and she could not locate the source.

Herynn knew her calf was still out there. She refused to listen to the others of her pod. They told her it was a phantom newborn echoes. They told her she was still grieving and needed more time to accept the loss.

Herynn would not believe this and refused to comply. There were days when she would leave the pod and search for her newborn. Though the matriarch knew the term newborn no longer applied. Over two seasons had passed and Okent would have grown.

But Herynn would occasionally hear the squeals of a newborn and not knowing who was making them would bring her sorrow. She would wander away from the others and weep. Many of the other mothers would chirp and click to her as if to provide solace. Herynn was grateful, but nothing would console her.

The orca pod continued to grow, and many newborns joined the group. There were times when younger males would leave the pod to start their own families, this was very natural and often the pods would meet up to hunt seals, sting rays and squid.

Herynn was a perfect aunty; she loved all the newborns and delighted in watching them grow. The other mothers encouraged Herynn to try for another newborn. They felt enough time had passed and a little one would add some distraction to the pain and loss occupying her life.

Herynn still felt it was not yet time. She would continue to hope to find her lost Okent. When she would catch a familiar sound and try to follow it, she would encounter other orcas. She would ask the pod members for any news of a lost newborn. Herynn knew to say, "He would be a young adult by now." No one could answer her questions or direct her to any place they might have seen an orphan orca or her newborn.

Herynn decided to leave the pod and begin a search of all the known orca routes of the ocean. She would search as far north and as far south as she could. She would head east and west in hopes of finding any clue of Okent. Herynn knew she would have to journey to new parts of the ocean. She knew there were many places Okent could have traveled too. Hopefully he was not alone.

Herynn gathered with Joop and Joom. She explained her decision to find Okent. Her search will take her very far and it might be some time before she returns. The matriarch clicked and chirped to her older sons.

"You are both ordered to stay with the pod. Listen to your aunties and elders for advice. Herynn increased her tone with a loud chirp, "Protect the pod!" She left her pod two seasons to the day she gave birth to Okent.

Her thoughts were focused, and she had a plan. Herynn clicked to herself, "My Okent is out there, I need to know he is safe."

CHAPTER NINE
THE DEATH FISH

The great white shark rarely swims in packs. While males may hunt in a small pack, they usually swim solo. The females always swim alone and the only time a grouping of males and females might occur is during mating season.

Often, the males are brutalized by the females and have the scars and bite marks to prove it. The females mature around fourteen years of age. They will secrete pheromones and enter an estrus phase. The males have to be extra cautious and at the same time more assertive to get the females to mate.

Male sharks make their intentions known by biting the dorsal fin of a female and pushing her onto her back. If a female submits to mating, she will roll over and swim with her back downward. She will then allow the male to swim over her. He will insert his claspers into her, and they will swim in unison. When the act is complete, the male will move away from the female very quickly, as sometimes she will bite and tear at the fleeing male.

When the mating season has passed, great whites will disperse and return to the ocean depths to swim in solitude. The female sharks begin a year-long gestation and become ravenous. With a successful fertilization of eggs, the young will grow inside of her, all the while being nourished by the eggs that are not fertilized. Unfortunately, for smaller pups, they will become food for their bigger utero siblings.

A very large female great white moves on from the mating grounds. She must continue her never-ending forward motion. Her head sways back and forth, searching for the scent of prey. Her mouth always slightly open to allow water to pass over her gills. She can taste the ocean and sense the heartbeat of any nearby fish. Anything swimming is food to her. A fresh kill is preferred, but she would scavenge more because of her pregnancy.

Many months have passed, and her abdomen is showing signs of several pups growing inside her. The female shark has registered a fresh scent. There is new blood in the water. A sword fish is feeding on silver hake: slashing its bill back and forth, dicing its prey in half. Electrical pulses are picked up and homed in on.

Ahead is a possible meal. Anything that will cause the hunger in her stomach to stop will do. She gathers speed with a few thrusts of her tail. She strikes at the sword fish. Her prey is cut in two, just past its gill slits. The fish was then shaken and swallowed whole, and its head floated slowly to the bottom. But the meal was not enough, and her hunger continued. She is a perfect evolutionary creature; she swims, she hunts, and she reproduces.

A new morning has come, and the shark has picked up the scent of humpback pod. She is a hunter and is very skilled at the killing of young humpback whales. The female great white can strike and retreat before a mother whale can flick her enormous tail and injure her.

She will flank, bite, and retreat, allowing the calf to quickly bleed out, then move in to feed on the dead whale. She does all this without thinking, as it is just instinct driven by hunger. After millions of years of evolution, the great white shark has changed very little. Although not as large as her ancestors, she measures twenty-five feet in length and weighs just over two tons. She is a perfect ocean organism. Her only rival would be a shark of equal or greater size. She begins to stalk the humpback pod, not realizing she would soon meet her greatest adversary.

Chapter Ten
A Ghost Amoung Us

The bulls were the first to feel the emptiness of the ocean. The morning had come and the sky was glowing yellow. The pod grouped together on the surface and bobbed up and down for air and the warmth of the sun. The newborns and young were kept corralled in the middle of the pod for safety.

The bulls circled the pod and alerted the mothers and aunties of any concerns. Clicks and whistles went out and soothing tones were used so as to not cause alarm. The potential threats came and went all morning.

Anytime the bulls picked up on a source of danger they moved to investigate, but often there was no threat to be found. The bulls would then return to the pod and continue guarding the group.

The pod elders were on alert and while songs were sung of a gray ghost lurking nearby, nothing came of it. The elders continued their patrol.

Okent felt the tension in the pod and asked Babel what was happening. She assured Okent that they were safe; the pod protected their own. Okent knew this to be true but decided to investigate on his own. He quietly moved away from the pod. He floated behind the humpbacks about a hundred yards away and waited.

The orca felt an emptiness in the ocean. He felt no other life around him except the pod, but then Okent echolocated, and he saw a great shape. There was a certainty about its movements. The young orca chirped quietly to himself "Gray Ghost." This was the term he had heard from the bulls all morning.

She approached the pod to gather their scent in her snout. She would then abruptly turn away and move around the pod. There were a few times she darted very deep to avoid the bulls, they would swim over her head and find nothing of her. She was stalking her prey. She was a hunter of humpbacks.

The shark was ready to start her attack run. She would flank a small humpback and strike at its side as this area was not protected by the mother's pectoral fin or flukes. She chose her victim in an instant.

She began her run, moving with incredible speed, cutting through the water bearing right at her target. Her mouth would stretch open wider than possible as her jaws could hyper-extend. A shark's jaws are not attached to their skeleton, which is made of cartilage, so they can thrust their jaws outward as they bite down on their prey. Her maw was four feet wide, with the bite force of eight tons. The female great white rolled her black eyes backwards in their sockets preparing to strike.

She would be upon the calf in seconds, cutting into flesh and tasting her prey.

The shark felt a tremendous blow to her belly. Agony filled her tiny brain. She could not process what had just happened. The emptiness in her stomach was just gone. A gaping hole released her internal organs into the ocean. Her last vision was that of a black and white creature swimming away with her liver. She floated downward and upside down. She watched her young swim out of her abdomen. The great white was no longer the hunter, she was the hunted.

Okent knew just what to do. He was echolocating the ghost when he saw it begin its attack run. He darted just below the ghosts abdomen and struck. The young orca tore and shook the ghost's organs. He just knew to take the liver and swim away with his trophy. Okent doubled back to watch the ghost twitch and die.

He briefly saw smaller ghosts leave the dying beast and scurry away.

CHAPTER ELEVEN
OKENT'S MISTAKE

The elder humpbacks had witnessed the whole event. Some were shocked, and some relieved. There were so many conversations happening at the same time, and nothing could be understood. Many were shouting in disbelief of what they just saw. Some were frightened by the way Okent killed the shark. Clicks, low rumbles, and high whistles were mixed together, describing in awe what just happened. The adult mothers of the pod circled their young, and none of the humpbacks were sure what to do.

McKeel was first to address the pod. He thanked Okent for his deed of bravery. Okent had saved a newborn from certain death. McKeel expressed his appreciation and asked the pod to do the same.

There was hesitation from a few of the other adults, who were still in shock at the violence they had just witnessed. Then, a mother explained how frightened she had become of Okent, that kind of violence was unthinkable. She clicked then bellowed, "Okent's actions were not like a humpback, why did he not slap his flukes at the attacking predator? This was not necessary! Such aggression was not needed." Clicks and whistles rang out again in a mash of conversation. One pod member asked, "What if Okent were to attack a newborn in the same way?" Some chirped, "How can he be trusted?" Others clicked, "Will he always be capable of such aggression?" More shouting broke out among the pod.

Okent's victory over the gray ghost was cut short by all the disorder and confusion coming from the pod. Worry washed over Okent's mind. So, he swam on the outer edge of the pod. He decided it was best to move away until they had all calmed down. Okent's own thoughts were, *I had to save the newborn; I protected a member of the pod. Why are so many upset with my actions?*

A few days had passed, and no one was speaking to Okent. There was only McKeel and Babel to keep him company. Later that night McKeel gathered the adults of the pod together to discuss what to do. McKeel wanted to assure the pod that Okent was not a danger, and then he reminded everyone how hard the young orca was trying to be part of the pod.

There were a few positive words coming from the gathered humpbacks, and most of the pod agreed that Okent would never hurt a family member.

The bulls assured everyone that they would always be watchful of Okent. But this made little difference to a small group of mothers and aunties. They wanted Okent to leave the pod. They were just too fearful of Okent hurting a newborn or worse.

Babel spoke to the group of mothers and did her best to comfort them. "Okent is part of our family, he was protecting a younger sibling." But they could not be persuaded.

Okent floated a few hundred feet away from the pod. He could tell there was a problem. The orca could sense how nervous the other young whales had become around him. It was at that moment Okent decided it would be best if he left the pod. There would be no harmony in the pod if he stayed, and Okent felt that he was old enough to be on his own and maybe find others like himself. He thought, *perhaps I can start my own pod.*

Okent chose to quietly swim away. First, he drew in a very large breath of air and submerged. He paused for a moment and glanced back at the humpback pod. Okent regretted not saying goodbye to Babel. She saved him as a newborn, and he would be forever thankful.

This time of year, the pod would be moving north. Okent decided to swim south. He could still hear the discussions about him from the pod. No one noticed he had left the area. Okent would miss the safety of the pod, but over the past few months, he was beginning to feel a longing to find others like himself.

Okent had come to realize he was not a humpback whale; he was just adopted by a caring mother. Babel had raised him, taught him to hunt fish and squid. McKeel had taught him to be brave and adapt to the ocean rules. The orca knew this was the right thing to do.

Okent surfaced after a long time. He got his travel bearing's by looking at the sun and feeling the ocean breeze. The orca thought to himself, *there is much to see, I will go where no humpbacks are.* He drew in a breath of air and pumped his tail flukes up and down in time to the waves of the sea.

Chapter Twelve
ALONE IN THE WORLD

Several months had passed and Okent was thriving. His hunting skills improved and his strength and speed increased. His overall appearance became that of an adult male Orca: solid black on top, a white underbelly, and patch of white on either side of his head, near his eyes and behind his dorsal fin, often referred to as a saddle. These markings were meant to confuse prey, especially the eye patches as they would confuse the would be food.

Okent's dorsal fin itself was over three feet tall. He was very comfortable in the sea, moving wherever he wanted. The orca had encounters with many different ocean creatures. Some were friendly, some stayed away from him, and on occasion some would challenge him.

Okent had no fear of great white sharks. He knew their limitations and exploited the sharks' weaknesses. Hunger was never an issue, but swimming alone with no pod to belong to weighed on him. He missed Babel, and he missed McKeel. (*My mother, my father.*)

Okent became very familiar with his world. He would travel up the coastlines of Mexico and the United States. He would continue up north to Alaska then across the Baltic Sea and to the Sea of Japan before finally arriving back in Hawaiian waters.

There was a time near the Sea of Japan where Okent heard the strangest noises coming from the surface. He did not recognize the sounds reverberating through the water. There was a constant chugging noises resembling a whish....whish...whish sound in the water.

Okent clicked, chirped, and whistled but there was no response. He moved closer to the creature floating on the water, and he popped his head above the surface to spy the noise maker. The water around the creature looked like frothing black slime. Churning in the waves were bits of flesh. Seagulls charged at the flotsam. The taste was foul, and the orca could see globs of black smoke being coughed out of the intruders blowhole.

Okent could not palate the water as it moved past him. There was nothing to describe what the taste was like. Foul and rotten flesh followed this monster, and the orca could also taste an oily substance in the water as well. He quickly moved away from this enemy of the sea. Okent would be sure to never follow this thing again, and always avoid it at all costs.

The floating creature chugged away, whish...whish...whish growing quieter. This was another learning moment for the orca. Perhaps this was the floating metal beast McKeel had warned him about. Someday, when he met up with McKeel again, Okent would ask him.

The orca continued his journey, still alone and still searching for another of his kind. He was hungry, and felt like sea turtle tonight. They were not his favorite tasting prey; their meat was hard to get to and he preferred stingrays. Still, they provided a good chase because they could turn so quickly. Okent could use his echolocation to always find their hiding spots.

The orca used this as a natural sonar, using clicking noises that bounce off an object in the water to form pictures in his mind. There was a huge clump of seaweed floating ahead of him, and Okent saw several pacific green sea turtles hiding amongst the kelp.

The orca now knew where to find dinner. His flukes began to propel him forward. He would stalk the turtles from below. A half hour later Okent had a very full stomach.

CHAPTER THIRTEEN
TO SLEEP AND DREAM

O kent moved through his world with courage and curiosity. He explored the surface of the ocean, and the depths of the sea. More time had passed than Okent could remember. His size was averaging twenty-two feet in length, and his weight was eleven-thousand pounds.

Okent was a young adult orca now. He became an apex predator and was very good at hunting. His prey would vary on the time of year and his mood. He only hunted when hungry, never just for sport.

Okent still hadn't met another of his kind. He knew he was different but didn't know what he was called. He had figured out he was not a humpback. Okent knew he had more in common with the dolphins he sometimes encountered. They avoided him completely and Okent never knew why. He would click and whistle to them, but for some reason they always swam away very fast.

Okent was unaware of the idea of hunting prey for pleasure. Okent never hunted whale or seal. He could only be taught what to hunt for by his own kind.

Still, he never had a problem feeding himself. There were so many different kinds of fish to choose from. The sea was vast.

Okent's favorite meal was sharks' liver. He found them very tasty and very filling. The liver dinner was the only time Okent would not share his spoils with the smaller ocean life that followed him.

After an exceptional meal, Okent would slumber on the surface. He was aware of his surroundings at all times but could still doze. This ability is called unihemispheric sleep.

Okent, like all orcas and dolphins, can put one side of his brain to sleep while the other side keeps his body breathing and aware of possible threats. Okent could then put the other side of his brain to sleep and continue breathing all the while receiving enough rest. An orca's brain is highly developed which aids in their ability to communicate with others, form strong family bonds and become expert hunters. Orcas are always learning. Orca's dream regularly, most often a dream would entail a hunt or swimming with a mate. But Okent's dreams were different. He would dream of Babel and McKeel. Many nights he would wake calling for them, chirping and squealing, "Where are you? I miss the pod." The worst nightmares would be getting lost in a cove of kelp or still seeing those brown beady eyes of seals staring at him and poking his sides with their snouts.

Sometimes Okent would dream of the floating metal monster. CHUG! CHUG! CHUG! Whish! Whish! Whish! BANG! BANG! BANG! He would swim away from the lucid nightmare noise till he fully awoke. Those dreams were easily forgotten after a full belly of squid and stingray.

Okent would sometimes hear the songs of other whales. He knew they were not his adoptive family by listening to the clicks, whistle and songs they made. He never responded to any humpback pod. The orca liked to keep to himself because he knew he was different from the others in those distant pods. Okent would swim in a different direction to avoid any encounters.

CHAPTER FOURTEEN
HUE

On one early morning, Okent was gently awakened by clicks and whistles of an unfamiliar voice. It was the sound of humpback, but he did not recognize who was calling out. Okent felt his heart shudder with excitement. The words and tones were so familiar but different at the same time. He then swam toward the voice. He slowly moved his head side to side to home in on the distant sound.

The clicks and whistles were a distress call. Okent decided he would help. This could be a brother humpback in trouble, or even one like himself.

Okent pumped his tail flukes faster and faster. The sound of clicks and whistles were just over two miles away. Within minutes the orca was nearing the source of the distress call. The dialect he was hearing was odd, but as he approached the whale, the cry for help turned into a warning to stay away.

Okent was very surprised to find an adult humpback tangled in a mess of floating line and debris. The humpback was in great distress. There was not a lot of time left for the exhausted whale. The humpback struggled to the surface to take a breath. His fins were tied to his body and his flukes were wrapped in plastic line and nylon rope. A large fishing net was wrapped around his torso.

Okent clicked and whistled that he could help. The humpback responded with threats and warnings to stay away. He moved his tail flukes to face Okent. "Stay back! I still can hurt you black fin!" Okent had never heard that term before. "Why do you call me black fin? I am here to help you humpback." The distressed whale again issued a warning to back away. "Stay back black fin! Stay back!"

Okent swam in a circle around the humpback, but at a distance so as to not be struck by its very powerful tail flukes.

The whale had struggled for days with the load attached to his body. He would drown if he did not reach the surface. The humpback was exhausted and needed to take a breath. He tried to rise to the top of the water, but the weight of all the debris held him down. The whale would begin to sink then force his way back to the surface to take a small breath.

Okent watched the humpback try to ascend. He was a few feet from the surface but could not close the distance. The orca decided to take a chance and help the stricken humpback. He slowly dove below the whale and came up under his lower jaw. Okent gently pushed the humpback's head above the water. The humpback inhaled, taking in great breaths. It had been days since he completely filled his lungs with ocean air.

The orca held the whale in this position for five minutes at a time, only stopping when he needed a breath. Then he would return to the underside of the humpbacks jaw and repeat the gentle nudge to the surface.

Okent repeated this for an hour and the humpback had started to regain some of his strength. Then the orca came up with a solution to the whale's problem. Okent had figured out a way to free the humpback, he thought it was possible to tear through the lines with his teeth.

Okent clicked and chirped to the humpback that he could free him. He explained that he would have to chew and bite through the mass of ropes and lines. The humpback was angered by this plan. He struggled in his fish net jacket and tried to swim off, listing sideways and slowing to a stop. The whale clicked another warning to Okent to stay away. No black fin could help him.

The orca grew impatient and with head movements and loud clicks he barked orders to stay still. He moved toward the tangled mess. The humpback stopped moving and watched Okent tear at the lines and rope. The orca was very precise with his bites. He never broke the skin of the humpback. The whale soon felt a relief of pressure from his torso. The humpback's huge red-gray eye followed Okent's every move. The whale sensed the tugging of the nets wrapped around his body. Then the humpback felt the restraint slip off his whole body. He could see pieces of the net floating to the bottom. Next, his flukes were set free. There were slices in the humpback's tail from the rope cutting into his flesh. The wounds bled slightly but would eventually heal.

Okent apologized and clicked, "The wounds were not caused by me but the cuts are deep humpback." The whale knew the wounds were not of Okent's doing but out of stubbornness, said nothing.

The orca circled the humpback to examine its massive form. The whale's body was over forty feet in length. Not as big as Babel, but close. Okent could find no trace of the net or rope. Nothing else was left attached to the great whale. He would be able to swim and breathe normally again. The humpback surfaced and took a breath on his own. Huge puffs of air and ocean mist soared into the afternoon sky. The whale stayed on the surface for some time, regaining all its strength and plotting a direction away from the black fin.

Okent had not noticed the color of the humpback while he was wrapped in the ropes and nets. It was only when the whale was floating on the surface that the orca realized the humpback was completely white!

Every part of the whale was bright white; the fins, flukes and bottom side. Even whiter than the white on Okent's belly area.

He remembered McKeel would sometimes tease him about his coloring. *"Make up your mind young one, are you black or white?"*

The humpback noticed the orca was staring at him. Okent had popped his head above the surface of the water to see the humpback's top. "Still white!" he chirped to himself. "Bright white!" he whistled. Okent asked if the humpback was in pain.

The whale bellowed a low toned "yes!" Okent replied "I am sorry to hear that." After a long pause the humpback finally responded with "it's not of your doing."

Okent took in some air and submerged to circle the whale. He studied the humpback's entire body again. The whale had the same shape as a humpback. The orca quickly brushed against the whale's side, it even felt like a humpback too. Okent was just amazed to see such a strange color on a humpback, or rather a lack of color. Then he realized he was staring again and swam in a different direction.

The orca floated to the surface and glided over to the humpback's face. Okent looked into the whale's eye and chirped, "I am Okent. What are you called?" There was a moment of uncomfortable tension, and a few up and down motions of fins and flukes. Then the humpback clicked his name, "My name is Hue." Okent clicked, "Hoo?" "Hue!" the whale bellowed.

Okent continued his questioning of the humpback. He quickly chirped, "Why do you call me black fin? How did you get tangled? Where is your pod?"

The whale was hearing all Okent's questions but remained silent. The orca continued his inquiries, and became more excited at meeting a new humpback whale. Hue just listened to the black fin chatter. The orca's chirps and clicks filled the ocean around him.

Hue wished he would go away. Finally, Hue lost his temper and bellowed, "ENOUGH!"

Okent paused his clicking and just swam upside down around the humpback's head. He looked at the albino humpback and waited for Hue to speak again. He flipped over and hovered in front of Hue.

Okent encouraged the humpback to speak by moving his pectoral fin in circles. Hue's thoughts were racing; he had never spoken to a black fin before. He was taught at a young age that black fins were killers. Hue could remember his pod elders fending off black fin attacks. How strange that this creature rescued him, and now continues to ask unending questions.

It was Hue's turn for questions, and he began with the most obvious one to ask. "Why did you assist me black fin? Do you plan to feed me to your pod?" Then Hue reminded the orca that he would flick his flukes and crush the black fins back. Okent twisted about and spun in a circle, then blew bubbles. He was not frightened by the repeated threats. Okent knew how fast he was in the water. He could move out of the way of the whale's flukes very easily.

Hue asked, "Where is your pod black fin?" Okent blew more bubbles, and remained in a hovering position next to Hue's left eye. Hue blinked and stared at the orca. Neither one spoke for a few moments.

Hue then declared it was time to move on. He had not eaten in days and would search out a school of small squid or krill, anything to stop the emptiness inside his body. Hue slowly pumped his tail, swimming away from the black fin.

Okent, having heard what Hue said, blew more bubbles and darted away. Within minutes, he returned to the where the humpback was, carrying a large adult stingray in his mouth. The orca offered the stingray to Hue as a welcoming gesture to his area of the ocean. Orcas are known to share their food and Okent was no different. But Hue was not impressed with the offering and swam past the orca. Okent slowly turned, pumped his flukes and began to follow. Hue bellowed "Leave me be, black fin, leave me be."

Okent dropped the stingray and hovered in front of Hue. The orca clicked and chirped more questions. He did somersaults in the water near Hue's left pectoral fin. Then the orca stopped and just watched the albino whale.

Hue pumped his great flukes and dove deep. Okent hovered in place and followed the humpback with his eyes. The albino whale was still visible sixty feet down. Okent could see his white glowing skin. He watched the humpback turn upward and ascend to the surface. Hue's mouth was open to the sea.

Okent could see the whale's mouth was lined with baleen, a filter-feeding system that large whales use to scoop up tiny plants and animal life from the ocean water.

When Hue reached the surface, he clamped his mouth shut causing a tremendous splash. Then the whale forced all the water out its mouth and swallowed his meal of krill with a single gulp. Okent watched Hue do this for two hours. The albino whale consumed over three thousand pounds of krill, plant life and small fish. Then, Hue finally had a full stomach. Okent hoped the humpback's mood would improve.

Hue rested again, only to fall into a light slumber. He still watched the black fin swim about. Hue kept a cautious eye on the orca. The albino thought, *what a strange creature this black fin is*. He wanted to flick the orca with his flukes. He would kill the puny black fin and be done with this nuisance.

Hue's mind filled with guilt at this thought. The black fin did release him from the lines and nets. He ushered the assault out of his brain. The albino whale hoped the black fin would grow bored and just swim away instead.

Okent decided he was going to try and talk to the humpback again. Maybe Hue knew of Babel's pod, perhaps he might have even met McKeel on his seasonal migration route. The subject had been on Okent's mind for some time now.

Okent would try to continue the conversation. He approached Hue slowly, hoping to get the whales attention. Hue glared at him with his right eye, then with a low-toned click asked, "What do you want black fin?" Okent chirped and clicked. "Have you ever met Babel?" There was silence. "Do you know McKeel?" Hue responded, "I do not know other black fins." Okent clicked and chirped again. "They are not black fins; they are humpbacks like you." The orca continued with a strong protesting tone. "Babel is my mother, and McKeel is my friend." Hue scoffed at Okent. "I have never heard of such a thing.

Humpbacks and a black fin? in the same pod?" Hue bellowed, "Never!"

Okent swam around the whale's long body, chirping and clicking his story to the albino. Hue pretended not to listen, and slowly moved away.

Hue took a breath at the surface and floated there while the orca continued with his account. Okent explained all he could remember and how he was taught to be part of the humpback pod.

Hue finally spoke, "Why are you not with the humpbacks' now?" Okent was at a loss to explain. He paused awhile to gather his thoughts. Hue continued to float at the surface and take in great breaths of air. His exhalation was loud and forceful. Hue was growing annoyed at the black fin again. The albino whale made a few pumps of its tail and moved away. Okent followed him, then came up beside the whale's left eye. The orca began telling the story of the shark attack. He explained how the pod was being stalked for hours by... the orca paused then clicked, "a gray ghost."

Okent told Hue that he sensed something in the water near the pod. This uneasy feeling was justified in that all life in the area seemed to have vanished. Except for the humpback pod, there was no movement. The pod numbered thirty-three, not counting a recent newborn. Okent continued with the events that followed. "I floated behind the pod. Then I saw a flash of gray and white moving at an incredible speed. It was heading straight toward a newborn calf. The giant fish was going to attack this newborn, having flanked its exposed side."

Now, Hue continued to listen with great interest. The orca described his next move but could not explain how he knew to kill the threat. Okent explained, "I swam into the shark's belly, ripping and tearing at the intruders' insides."

The orca told Hue he stopped the shark attack within yards of the newborn. The orca chirped, "I then ate the shark's liver in a few bites."

Hue's eyes were wide open now, he thought to himself that *this young black fin risked its own life to save a newborn humpback whale.* Hue shifted his enormous body to better see the orca. He then asked the black fin what happened next.

Okent continued with his story, he spoke of the fear the pod developed toward him after seeing the attack. There was much discussion among the elders. The pod was divided by the results of the attack. Many were grateful and many were nervous. Okent ended his tale with his decision to leave the humpback pod and clicked, "That's how I came to be here and how I found you."

Hue had listened very intently. He had a respect for the orca's actions. The albino humpback told the black fin he understood both sides of the situation. Hue and the orca continued to talk. A full day had passed since Okent freed the tangled whale. Hue spoke of his departure from his own pod. A total of forty-five elder humpbacks and thirteen young ones.

Hue knew his body color could attract predators or worse. He convinced the elders that it would be best if he left the pod. The albino whale was doing what he thought best to protect his fellow humpbacks. There was a great deal of talk against Hue leaving the pod. In the end the albino decided to swim in a different direction than his humpback family.

Okent asked, "What could be worse than a predator?" Hue explained, "There are beasts that float on the water, and they have the ability to kill from the surface. The beasts could send pointed tooth-bone sticks through the water, striking the bodies of whales, biting into their flesh and locking in place. These tooth-bones would cause great pain and extreme blood loss." Hue clicked quietly, "This always had a fatal outcome."

He continued, "A whale that was struck would cry for help, but there was nothing to be done. Then the whale would bleed out so quickly it could not fight the beast. The ocean became a red froth of water and death. The floating beast would take the whale from the ocean into its waiting mouth never to be seen again. A horrible taste was left in the water as the beast moved away from the surviving whales."

Okent was stunned by Hue's story. This was exactly what McKeel had explained to him. These floating beasts were deadly. More dangerous than even sharks. Okent told Hue he had heard of these beasts before. He was made aware of the danger from his friend McKeel. Hue was not surprised by Okent's statement and clicked, "This McKeel is a wise humpback, I hope to meet him someday." Okent took this as a good sign. Hue was opening up to him.

The albino bellowed, "Black fin! It is time to feed again!" The emptiness from hunger was back in both their bellies. Hue told Okent to follow him and watch what he does very carefully.

Okent watched the albino whale gather food into its enormous mouth and close its jaws together while expelling hundreds of gallons of ocean water. In a single swallow, the whale's mouth was empty. Hue began to repeat his skillful way of eating again and again.

Okent responded by catching food the same way, but with a little more of a hunting style. Okent would swim under a school of fish and blow bubbles to round them up. He would then turn on his side to flash the white skin part of his belly. This would startle the fish to swim closer together and rise to the surface. Okent would float under the school, and with a few pumps of his flukes he would scoop up a mouth full of whatever fish had gathered.

Hue had watched Okent intently. He commented on Okent's skill as an excellent hunter and asked where he learned to hunt like this. Okent explained that Babel had taught him. But Okent added that he also used his own technique to catch fish. The orca chirped, "Everything I know, I learned from Babel and McKeel." Hue clicked with a sympathetic tone, "Perhaps you will meet them again someday." Okent paused, then clicked, "I miss them both very much, I miss the safety of my pod."

There was a quiet peace between the albino and the orca. They spent the rest of the evening feeding and making friendly conversation. That night, many stories were exchanged. Okent spoke of his travels and exploring areas of the ocean he had never heard of from his pod. Hue spoke of the similar adventures, and always avoiding other pods. The albino had no fear of gray ghosts, just like the black fin. He could easily crush them with his tail flukes. Without knowing it, the albino and the orca were becoming friends. They both dozed on the surface of the ocean. No moon could be seen in the evening sky. It was very dark on the ocean that night.

CHAPTER FIFTEEN
FOLLOW ME SOUTH

The morning had returned, and Hue began to stir. The seagulls were flocking around the two of them. The gray and white birds were scavenging bits of fish floating about the whale and the orca. Hue found the creatures loud and bothersome. Occasionally he swallowed one that would not move away from the krill and fish he was consuming. Soon after, Hue would spit the dead bird out feeling no remorse. Okent chirped and clicked to the humpback. They both exchanged glances and then a nod.

Hue was the first to speak in a full sentence. His clicks and chirps were so much louder than the orca's. Okent thought about saying something about this but decided not to.

Hue began, "Black fin! I have thought about this through the night. I think it would be wise if we travel together. We can be our own pod. Together we are safer and gathering food would be a simpler task." Okent hovered and blew a bubble stream from his blowhole. "What say you black fin?" Okent answered, "Where will we go first?" The albino responded, "Anywhere we choose." The orca chirped. "Then pick a direction." Hue bellowed "SOUTHWEST!" The two adventurers began their journey. They headed southwest for days, only stopping to feed and sunbathe, with occasional breaching.

The coast of Japan was before them and Hue and Okent could hear other whales in the area. They remained silent, not communicating with other pods.

On two occasions the albino and the orca heard and tasted the foulness of the floating beast. The taste of death and the black slime followed the wicked creature. The two companions knew to avoid the beast. They dove very deep and waited for the horrid creature to move away from them.

Hue spoke of a plan to kill the beast. He would bash at it with his flukes and Okent could tear at its belly. The orca agreed the beast had to die, but expressed that they would need many more like themselves to actually kill it. Hue knew the orca was correct. Hue clicked a long low tone: "Someday beast, someday."

Much time passed, as the two companions swam together. They made sure, to always keep within communication distance. They even developed their own way of speaking. Clicks and chirps were understood between them, as were whistles, and bubbles were also used. Hue continued to make songs, which Okent enjoyed. The orca could never figure out exactly what Hue was singing about and sometimes his songs lasted for hours.

Days turned to months, and then a whole season had passed. Their ocean journeys took them further and wider than any other pod had traveled. The humpback and the orca discovered new places and new routes. The ocean currents were simple to navigate and provided many sources of food.

This time of year, the two companions were west of the Marianna Islands. The course would take them just north of Japan. They would then head south along the coast of Japan. The ocean temperature was warmer than usual, for early spring. Okent made the comment and rhetorically asked why different parts of the ocean had different temperatures. Okent, just like Hue, preferred to swim in cooler waters. They would move south sooner than later.

CHAPTER SIXTEEN
BLOOD COVE

The albino whale was a few hundred yards ahead of the orca. Hue paused and floated while the orca dove on a fever of Mobula sting rays. The orca then returned to the surface with a ray. Okent exhaled, then took in a breath. Hue thought to himself, *that the black fin never misses.*

The albino humpback always knew his exact location. Even in unfamiliar waters Hue could figure out his place in the ocean. Okent was learning new skills of plotting direction and course routes from the albino. He was happy to share his knowledge. Okent was a solid friend and a quick study.

Hue figured they were now two miles east off the coast of Japan. This early morning Hue started to hear horrible screams, very far off. He informed the orca of these cries of terror. Hue described the calls of help to be filled with agony and it hurt him to hear.

Okent asked, "Should we go help? Is there something we can do?" He said, "Let us find out." Hue pumped his enormous tail flukes and headed toward the shore. The two companions could hear the death cries of many, many creatures. There was a great amount of blood floating in the water. This blood was like none Okent had ever tasted before. He asked the humpback, "What is this blood, Hue? Who is it coming from?"

Hue stopped swimming a few hundred yards from shore. He did not want to get cut by the rocks or stranded on the beach. Okent glided up next to him.

The albino and the orca popped their eyes above the water. In the cove ahead of them, they saw an unimaginable event. The ocean water all along the beach was completely red.

It was the blood of at least three hundred adult dolphins. The two companions watched in shock at what was happening. They could not look away. The cries they heard began to overwhelm their ears. Hue was sure he spotted small whales, but a different species than humpback.

There were tiny wood shells floating around the dying creatures. A long net held them close to shore. The whale spied upright mammals stabbing at the dolphins with long tooth-bone sticks. They would bite into the dolphins' necks and blood would flow from the wound.

Hue became enraged; he began swimming in circles and then breaching repeatedly. He cried out, "STOP THIS! STOP IT NOW!"

Okent felt Hue's rage and heartbreak as well, but there was nothing either of them could do. The killing area was too close to shore. Neither whale nor orca could reach the suffering dolphins.

Hue bellowed again, while the orca breached and twisted in the air. The walking mammals noticed the commotion offshore and just stared. A few moments later they returned to stabbing the defenseless dolphins.

The albino bellowed, "Black fin! We must leave NOW!" Hue could not take any more of this atrocity. He headed out to sea, and when he could, he dove very deep.

Hue wanted to be in the darkness of the ocean.

CHAPTER SEVENTEEN
PORPHYRIOUS

A week had passed for the two companions. Hue barely spoke and had not eaten since blood cove. This was the term Hue would mumble to himself whenever the orca tried to talk to him.

Okent was growing more concerned for Hue. The orca spent the days floating and swimming a small distance from Hue. He thought it was best to give the albino space and time. Okent knew that Hue would speak when he was ready. Hue would often sink very deep and position his body head down, tail up. Okent knew that humpbacks do this to sleep sometimes. The whale would stay like this for hours. Perhaps it was Hue's way of recovering from the trauma they both witnessed. Okent was still feeling numb from what he had seen, but found comfort in eating large amounts of squid. Okent would be patient with Hue for as long as it took. The ocean was peaceful and there were little to no waves and perhaps it was a good thing to let Hue relax for a while.

A few days later Hue began to speak. Low tones and sad songs were his soliloquy. Okent tried to understand the albino's words, but nothing made sense to him. Hue began to swim close to the surface and he even peeked an eye above the waves. Okent quietly chirped and whistled to his albino friend. "We are very far away from that place. We shall never return to that cove." Hue clicked a "yes" and then bellowed, "AGREED!"

Hue began to make small talk with Okent again. He expressed his appreciation to the orca for remaining by his side. Hue stopped swimming and hovered just below the surface of the water. He took in a breath of ocean air. He looked at Okent and was getting ready to speak. The orca realized that just like McKeel, the humpback always considered his words before speaking them.

Hue began to tell a story. "This tale is about revenge and justice." The orca thought, *those two words do not really belong together*, Okent knew it was one or the other. The orca decided to listen without interrupting the humpback. He said, "This story was passed down to me from my elders and their elders."

Long ago before the time of time, there was a great whale, much larger than myself. The great whale was deeply wronged by the land-walking mammals. They would hunt his kind and they would kill members of his pod. The great whale was called Porphyrious. This whale refused to allow these injustices to continue so he began to hunt the land-walking mammals in their floating wood shells. No matter the size of these wood shells, Porphyrious would charge and smash them to bits and then swallow the land-walking-mammals that survived his attack. He sank many wood shells and killed many land-walking mammals. Porphyrious was a hero among all the ocean's whales. In time, the land-walking mammals stopped their hunting of whales and stayed close to shore. They fished for herring and mackerel and let the whales live in peace."

Hue paused as he rose to the surface to take a breath. Okent waited for the albino to continue the story. He spoke again after a little while; "If I ever encounter the land-walking creatures in my ocean, I will kill them. I will smash their floating wood shells, no matter the size."

Hue was done telling his story to the orca. He then turned and swam east following the equator. Hue always knew where he was in the ocean. Okent felt more at ease now that Hue had spoken, and hoped the albino would feed soon. The two companions continued their journey, and Hue began to sing as he followed the earth's magnetism. Okent wondered what the albino was singing about but decided not to ask.

Several days passed, and Hue had begun to feed again. Okent had just filled his own belly when a memory flickered through his head. The ocean water tasted familiar and the temperature was to the orca's liking. This reminded Okent of his pod life. Many seasons had passed since he last saw his mother and friend.

That night, while resting on the surface, Okent had vivid dreams, waking him from a deep slumber. The orca shifted about and began to doze again.

Okent was dreaming of his birth mother. The orca clicked and whistled, he chirped then squealed. Splashing the sea surface, he woke suddenly and called her name. "Herynn?!"

Hue opened an eye to look at Okent. The orca was quiet for a moment, then said to Hue, "My birth mother's name is Herynn."

Chapter Eighteen
The Matriarch

Herynn had spent three seasons searching the coastlines and the great ocean routes. She followed the currents north, west, south, and east. Sometimes Herynn would meet other family pods of orcas and stay with them for months, always showing proper respect to the matriarch of each pod.

Time was a concern for her so when the opportunity presented itself, Herynn would bid them goodbye. With a pump of her flukes, she was off to continue the search for her offspring Okent.

Her most recent encounter with a large orca pod gave her the strangest clue of Okent. Members of this particular pod spoke of a sole orca traveling with a humpback whale. Not just any humpback, but a pure, white-skinned whale. Herynn knew this to be unheard of in the ocean world. She was shocked to hear this and leery to believe. The elders spoke of other pods witnessing the two companions swimming together. The orca and humpback would always stay a great distance away from others. They would ignore all communication attempts made by orca pods. Sensing that the two wanted to be left alone, no one followed them.

The matriarch was then given a course to follow, and she explored the possibility that this lone orca could be her Okent. Herynn knew she had traveled further than her own family pod had ever gone. Whenever she met new orca pods, they would demonstrate different hunting techniques. Herynn would master the tactics quickly. She would then teach the new pod her own hunting style. Someday Herynn would return to her family pod and teach them what she had learned. She could feed the young ones and at the same time show them how to capture food.

The lone matriarch had made her way to the tip of South America. There are many orca pods in the area of Patagonia. She heard the conversations of a group of female orcas hunting porpoise. She swam in their direction.

Herynn announced herself and was immediately greeted by the other orcas. Several members of the pod circled her and expressed a very warm greeting. Some orcas would slap their flukes against the surface of the water, while others would rub up against her. There was a great deal of excitement in meeting the traveler. The younger orcas were curious and asked many questions. Clicks and whistles, squeals and chirps were directed to Herynn. "Where are you from? Can you teach us any games? What is your favorite food to hunt?" Herynn was quick to answer all their questions.

Then there was a sudden quietness from the pod. Their matriarch swam into Herynn's view.

With grace she approached the traveling orca and introduced herself. "I am Vess. You are welcome to swim with us. You are welcome to hunt with us. What are you called?" The visiting orca warmly replied, "I am Herynn."

Vess was about the same size as Herynn but had more weight. She had some scars about her body, most likely from battling sharks. The two female orcas were both twenty-eight feet in length but had slightly different markings.

Herynn knew depending on the area of the ocean, orcas would have different coloring. Herynn could tell Vess was older, and much wiser.

Vess made clicking and chirping sounds, and squeals that she did not recognize. Herynn knew that orca pods had their own dialect and it would be just a short amount of time before she figured out the new pods' language.

Having heard Vess's directions, three younger orcas darted away and returned in minutes to present their guest with a choice of stingray, squid or whale blubber.

Vess spoke again, "You must be famished. Have you traveled far?" Herynn was more than happy to take the whale blubber. She nibbled at the fresh meat and continued to talk with Vess."I have," chirped Herynn. Vess continued, "We hunted a gray whale yesterday and the kill is very fresh. The whole pod has eaten, please take as much as you wish."

Herynn was very appreciative of the whale blubber. She knew that the elders of the pod were the only members strong enough to hunt a gray whale. An orca pod could stalk a whale of great size and when the time was right move in for the kill. The hunt is carried out with a team effort. Male and female orcas will move as a pack and each orca has a role to perform. The prey is followed to the point of exhaustion. Small nips are taken from the whales' body. The orcas do this to taste their prey and start a blood trail. The other pod members use their echolocation to follow the whale. The prey is spied on from above and below the water. When the whale can't defend itself any longer, the abdomen becomes an easy target. This is where an orca pod will strike. Orcas will take turns smashing into the soft areas of the whale, inflicting internal damage with each blow. Then they will repeatedly slap the whale with their powerful tail flukes. The teenagers of the pod are encouraged to join in the hunt, while the youngest members watch and learn. All hunting techniques are shared and learned by family members. The survival of the pod is paramount.

The visiting orca missed the taste of blubber. She would not be capable of killing a whale by herself. Perhaps a wounded or young whale, but not one of great size. She delighted in her meal and enjoyed her new surroundings. After she had her fill of blubber, Herynn's thoughts turned to Okent.

Herynn knew he would be about twenty five feet in length by now. She hoped he was healthy. It has been many years since she lost him, but she would continue to search for him in a few days. Herynn would speak of her offspring tomorrow. She would ask of any sightings of an orca and a white humpback traveling together. Strange as that may sound, a clue could be given. This coupling of orca and humpback still seemed very unnatural to Herynn.

The visiting matriarch wanted to become familiar with Vess's family members first, so that night Herynn gathered with the other orcas. They all slumbered in a group while a few elders patrolled the perimeter of the pod. The young were corralled into the middle of the group for safety. Misty breath came from all their blowholes. Orcas can control the muscular flap that seals the blowhole watertight. They're conscious breathers, so they must remember to breathe. The pod was just below the ocean surface, and with little effort could pop their head above the water to take a breath. During the day when they are most active, an orca will usually submerge for five to ten minutes then surface for a breath.

Herynn took in the stars, and breathed in and out with the oceans movement. On this night Herynn would sleep and dream of all her offspring. Wherever they may be, she wished them all well.

Herynn woke ready for the hunt. She began to hear the pod stir. There were chirps and whistles of "good morning." Then the pod readied itself for the hunt. Vess whistled and chirped commands.

Herynn determined that the pod was very far from shore and asked why. Vess explained to the visiting matriarch the reasoning behind the distance. "We don't want to let our prey know we are nearby." She advised Herynn that the best way to learn would be to watch. Vess was going to teach her to catch sea lions on shore today. This hunt would be very special, but dangerous.

CHAPTER NINETEEN
NOT SAFE ON SHORE

Six female orcas lined up next to Vess, and they swam in unison towards the beach. Many sea lions had positioned themselves on the shoreline. All thought they were safe on land. The bravest of the sea lions would spring into the ocean to catch a fish or crab, then climb back onto the beach.

Their movements were being observed by the female orcas. Vess would begin her run only when she determined her attack approach. The first attempt was the only strike an orca could use and Vess had to be precise. If she missed her prey, it would be a while before the sea lions returned to the ocean. The attack would scatter the sea lions further up the beach, away from the waves. She had to be on mark and ride the wave in.

Vess hovered and took a quiet breath of ocean air.

The wise matriarch made her move, pumping her flukes in time with the top of a wave. Vess rode the water stream just below the cress, her bulbous head blended with the shape of the wave. Her eyes locked onto a sixty pound sea lion making its way onto the beach. Waves crashed around the oblivious seal. In a remarkable act of agility Vess swam sideways to hide her dorsal fin. She slightly twisted her mouth down and snatched the sea lion off the beach. She clamped down on the wiggling mammal and turned her massive body toward the open sea. Vess applied all her strength to her fins and flukes to move away from the beach as quickly as possible. Within moments her body was submerged in the ocean and she was heading back to the pod with her prize. The creature struggled against the orca's bite, but it was useless, as the sea lion was being held firm by the orcas conical shaped teeth. Vess sensed her prey was on the brink of shock. She let go of her prize. The sea lion, being disoriented, swam in a circle. Confusion flooded the small mammal's brain.

Vess swam just under her prey and as she did, she snapped her tail and sent the sea lion hurling through the air, twisting, and somersaulting till it hit the water. The sea lion was stunned and bleeding. The rest of the pod moved around the injured creature and flung it into the air again. It was dead before it crashed into the ocean for a fourth time. Playtime was over and the pinniped became a meal for the pod.

Herynn watched and took in everything. The visiting matriarch would make her own attempt at catching this tasty prey. Her first beach attack was about to happen. She timed her run with the cress of a wave, keeping pace with the kinetic energy in the water. Her massive body was being propelled toward the beach. Herynn approached her prey with great accuracy and stealth. She slightly twisted her body sideways and opened her jaws. Then, feeling the creature enter her mouth; she clamped down on its body.

Herynn immediately turned her head left and started pumping her flukes with all her strength. Her pectoral fins aided in the movement of her twelve-thousand-pound body. Herynn's skin was smooth and wet, so she easily moved over the sand. Less than a minute later she was fully submerged and heading away from the shore. The sea lion was struggling against its capture, and fighting to breathe. Herynn ended its life as she approached the pod. No playing with her meal was needed. She presented the sea lion to a group of orcas as a thank you for accepting her into their pod. The youngest orcas chirped and whistled while they enjoyed their breakfast.

CHAPTER TWENTY
SHE ALREADY KNOWS

The sunset was less than an hour away and the shore hunt was successful. The pod was fed, and many games were played. Now was the time to rest. Members of the pod gathered in smaller groups to discuss the hunt. Chirps and clicks went back and forth, followed by exhaled puffs of misty air. Others celebrated in having full bellies with leaps and tail flaps. Many were impressed with how quickly Herynn learned to snatch prey from the shore.

Vess had gathered with her most trusted elders a short distance from the pod. Herynn wondered if this was a proper time to discuss her situation. She floated nearby waiting for the opportunity to approach Vess.

The wise matriarch noticed Herynn and chirped to her that she may come closer. Without hesitation she swam to the group. Vess began the conversation before Herynn could say a word. "I understand you are looking for your lost offspring, he has been missing for some time." Herynn clicked and chirped, "Yes, this is true."

Vess continued, "Many pods have spoken of a white humpback traveling with a sole orca. Could this be your lost one?" There was a quiet in the ocean now. Herynn paused then responded, "I believe it may be; how have you heard of this?"

The matriarch chirped, "I am Vess."

At that moment Herynn realized that Vess was a grand matriarch of many pods. She was the leader of a whole clan of orcas. This was a great responsibility to hold. Her understanding of the ocean and the many orcas in the sea was vast. Herynn had never met a grand matriarch, and was greatly honored by Vess to be accepted into the pod.

Vess spoke again, "I will send word to all the pods in the ocean to report any sightings to me. I ask that you wait a few more sunsets before you continue your search."

Herynn felt a wave of hope wash over her. With such a far reach and a possible clue she may finally learn of Okent's location. Herynn was humble before the grand matriarch and expressed her gratitude.

The next day could not come fast enough. Herynn returned to the main pod, while Vess chirped directions to her trusted elders. She watched them all disperse in different directions with great speed. Members of the pod circled Herynn to comfort her, as they were all aware of her search. The youngest orcas caressed her sides as they swam past her. There were many chirps and clicks of encouragement. Herynn heard the word "soon" being chirped several times.

CHAPTER TWENTY-ONE
THE GREATEST OF WHALES

Hue and Okent had just weathered a small storm. They stayed close for safety and comfort, only coming up for air when needed. Hue knew that Okent had to surface more often and respected the black fin's ability to stay positive through the whole event. The waves were annoying but tolerable.

As the sea settled down, the two companions floated at the surface and started to feed. Okent came back with a seagull in his mouth. The seagull in turn had a large fish in its beak. The orca came across the bird diving for mackerel and took advantage of the situation. Okent thought, *two for one!* Hue bellowed his disgust for the creature. "I spit them out, not enough flesh on their bones."

Okent responded "It will do for now; I will stalk a sea turtle in a moment." Hue looked at the black fin puzzled, "How do you always know where your prey is before you see it?" Okent just blew a few bubbles as if to say, *I have explained this to you many times, old friend.* Hue got the message with the bubbles floating by his right eye.

Okent swallowed the bird (and fish) and quickly darted away from the albino whale. The orca began using his echolocation ability and homed in on a large sea turtle floating amongst the kelp. He picked up speed and silently scooped up the sea turtle into his mouth before the sea mammal realized he was a meal for the orca. Okent finished the sea turtle by cracking its shell and swallowing its insides. This one happened to be a female full of eggs. But the orca felt no remorse and enjoyed his meal. Okent snatched up another sea turtle and headed back to Hue. The albino did not like to be apart for too long. He picked up speed and clicked to Hue, that he was on his way back. "I will be there soon; I hope you had your fill. Should we move north?"

Hue began to respond, but just as a click went out to the black fin, the humpback stopped his message. He paused and took in the ocean's lack of life sounds. There was a great emptiness; the sea was void of all noise, no chatter coming from anywhere. Complete silence surrounded the albino humpback. A powerful shudder ran through Hue's entire body. Hue's brain alerted him to a great beast heading toward Okent. The humpback bellowed as loud as he could, he cried out to the orca to swim! "Swim very fast, swim to me with all your strength, NOW!"

Okent heard Hue and at the same time felt the emptiness in the ocean. The orca bolted with incredible speed toward his traveling companion. He swam in a defensive pattern, alternating his direction ever so slightly to avoid what was chasing him but it was no use; Okent felt the presence behind him. He had no ability to see what it was. The orca could feel a tremendous wave of pressure building behind him. The wave caught up to him an began to move him off course. Hue had begun swimming toward the orca, pumping his powerful tail flukes to get to Okent.

Hue could see what was chasing Okent now and knew he had to stop the impending collision but the albino was a moment too late. He saw Okent pitch up to the surface as the great beast smashed into him from behind. The orca breached the ocean almost sideways and still pumping his tail flukes. Okent flailed in the air and smashed down onto the water upside down.

The beast swam in a half circle and began to charge Okent again. This time Hue was there to block the sperm whale's direction. "STOP! STOP NOW! STOP your attack on the black fin! STOP!" Hue bellowed the words to the great sperm whale and positioned himself bravely in front of the largest toothed cetacean in the ocean. The attacker slowed and approached the albino. The sperm whale clicked and bellowed to Hue in the loudest voice the albino had ever heard. "Why do you protect the black fin? He is a killer of our young and old." The albino looked around for Okent, but he was nowhere to be seen. Hue paused longer than he should have while speaking to a creature of such size and strength.

Hue was full of rage and concern for his companion. He looked at the sperm whale's right eye with his left. The attacking whale was at least seventy feet in length and had a bottom jaw lined with conical-shaped teeth. Hue could see the battle scars all along the sperm whales' mouth and sides. The scars were from the many tentacle suction cups containing a claw that a colossus squid would use to fight off a predator. The humpback knew the huge squid had a razor-sharp beak and could bite through flesh and bone. Hue avoided the creatures when they were near the surface which was extremely rare. They are deep-sea swimmers, and they prefer the dark and the cold of the ocean.

Hue finally answered, "Why have you attacked the black fin? He is not a threat to you." The humpback had used extremely harsh tones in his clicks and chirps. The albino had never been this angry in all his seasons.

The great sperm whale moved closer to the humpback and spoke, "Answer me before I smash you." Hue moved into a threating position as well. The humpback knew he was thirty feet less in length but would still fight with long-ago learned fighting skills. Both whales readied themselves for battle. The albino could see the anger in the great bull's eye.

Hue shouted again at the gray beast "Why are you so full of anger? How have you been wronged? Speak to me now sperm whale!"

The great whale was seething with rage. Its eyes were bloodshot and fierce. Hue could tell he would be attacked at any moment. It was not too late to flee and look for Okent. The gray bull broke right and was preparing to smash into the albino.

"Loutt! Stop this now! Loutt, Hear me!" The great whale turned to the voice calling to him. A smaller female sperm whale approached the dueling cetaceans. She swam between her mate and Hue. She gently brushed the great sperm whale and sang in soothing tones. "Loutt, please stop." Hearing his mate's song and clicks, the sperm whale settled into a submissive position. He hovered next to her, and they rubbed their pectoral fins together. "I am Sprek. Are you injured, humpback?" Hue took in the situation and thought of Okent. He replied, "Why have you attacked my companion?" Loutt bellowed, "He is a black fin!" Hue clicked, "I must go find him." Sprek responded, "We can help you." Loutt clicked, "I will not, we must get back to her." Hue could hear Okent clicking and chirping far away from his position. The albino humpback chirped, "I must go, I do not need your help." As Hue was turning toward Okent's calls, Sprek spoke to him again. "We may need your help."

Hue was curious and clicked to Sprek. "Speak fast, I must find my companion and make sure he is not injured." Loutt responded, "I barely touched the orca; he was too agile and turned too fast. I could see he was unharmed." The three whales hovered near the surface taking in quick breaths of air. Then Sprek clicked to the albino, "It would be best to show you." Hue resolved, "Then show me quickly."

CHAPTER TWENTY-TWO
CAMISS

The great whales turned together and swam east of their position. Hue paused, then followed them. He sent clicks to Okent to wait for him. "I will find you black fin." Hue kept a space between himself and the sperm whales.

After a short distance they stopped and hovered just under a large seaweed patch. Sprek clicked and sang a short song. Hue recognized the words as, "It is safe now, you may come out."

The humpback heard a small voice reply, "Mother? Father?" from the floating patch of kelp, a young female sperm whale descended. She moved very slowly and with great caution. Sprek approached her offspring and caressed her side. Loutt came up on the opposite side and nuzzled his daughter.

Hue could see the young whale was hurt. He slowly swam closer to her to see the extent of her injury. The young sperm whale was comforted by her parents as Hue approached. The humpback swam the length of her body on both sides. When he was halfway down her right-side Hue could see a tooth-bone stick protruding from her mid-section. The stick part was broken away, leaving just the tooth-bone jutting out of her skin. There was a small flow of blood coming from the wound. The young female was in great pain. Fortunately, the tooth-bone was not too deep. The only way the wound would heal would be to remove the tooth-bone. Hue knew his own mouth lacked teeth to grip the tooth-bone, and his tongue would not be any help either. But Hue did know who could help. He would explain his idea to Loutt and Sprek. The albino asked the young female, "What are you called?"

She clicked, "I am Camiss." The humpback used a comforting tone and clicked, "I am Hue, I will not harm you, I have an idea to help you." Hue turned to face Camiss' parents. I have a story to tell you about why I am befriended to the black fin.

Hue began his story but shortened it a bit, as he wanted to retrieve Okent's help quickly: "I was trapped in line and net, and I could not ascend to the surface to breath and I was exhausted. I called for help and the black fin responded. I warned him to stay back, but he persisted. The black fin, using his teeth and tongue, bit through the tangled ropes and line. After a short while the debris fell from my body and floated to the ocean floor. I could swim freely again. I could feed again. The black fin saved my life."

Loutt bellowed, "Why do you tell us this? Is this black fin capable of helping Camiss?"

Hue answered the great sperm whale with a simple "yes." Then continued, "I will find Okent and explain to him about your daughter's situation. I think he will help her." Then the albino turned from the sperm whales and said, "I will be back, please wait here and be patient for my return, Camiss."

The young sperm whale quietly thanked the humpback with a nod and clicked "I will wait for you here."

Hue started singing to Okent, and he explained through clicking and squeals that he was looking for him. "Please tell me where you are old friend."

In the distance Okent began to chirp and squeal, he was resting near the surface breathing in time to the waves, "I am right here." and then Okent added another few clicks, "I have something to ask you."

CHAPTER TWENTY-THREE
OKENT FINDS A WAY

The albino found the black fin floating on the surface and asked his condition. The orca chirped, "I am unharmed but my body feels numb." Then Okent asked, "What was chasing me, Hue?"

The humpback swam a circle around the orca, checking for injuries. He moved close to the orca, looking him in the eye, "You, my friend were attacked by a sperm whale, the largest I have ever seen or heard of."

Okent blew bubbles and thought *how strange.* "Why me, Hue?" the albino responded, "Because you are black fin, you are known to hunt his kind for pleasure. A pod of black fins can easily kill a young sperm whale or even a female sperm whale."

Okent was beginning to feel sensation in his fins and flukes again. "I will confront this sperm whale; I am not a killer of ones like you, my friend."

Hue clicked, "I know this black fin, but others do not. It is part of the reason why we swim alone."

Okent knew the humpback's logic was sound. Hue continued, "Black fin, there is a situation that only you can help with, please listen carefully. I have met the attacking sperm whale and his family." Hue paused then continued, "I have come from them with a request for a service."

Okent just stared at the albino. Then he squealed, "What did you just say?" Hue clicked an inpatient sounding response to the orca, "Their offspring is injured; and it is mostly why you were attacked." The orca clicked and chirped. "I do not understand, I was attacked by them and now they request my help?" Hue bellowed, "Allow me to explain, black fin!"

Okent swung upside down and blew bubbles, as he always did when Hue was in a tense mood. It seemed to lighten the whales demeanor. The humpback told the orca of Camiss and her injury. "You, black fin, must pull the tooth-bone out. Only your mouth and teeth are capable." Hue clicked "Will you help her, Okent?"

The orca asked Hue, "Will the great sperm whales allow me near their offspring?" Hue answered quickly. "I believe they will, now we must go."

The two long time companions swam in the direction of the sperm whales. Hue was in communication with Camiss's parents. The albino announced their approach with short songs and clicks. Loutt and Sprek greeted the humpback and the orca a few hundred feet away from where their offspring was floating.

Loutt wanted a proper inspection of the orca and a formal introduction. All this was expected from a creature so much smaller than him. Sprek pushed away from her mate and introduced herself to Okent. "I am Sprek. Are you here to help my offspring?" Okent spoke respectfully to Sprek and asked to be introduced to Camiss.

The female sperm whale gave a soft touch to her mate with her pectoral fin. Then she clicked to Okent, "Please follow me black fin."

The orca swam next to the female sperm whale and glared at Loutt. The great sperm whale stared menacingly back at Okent. The orca clicked and chirped very loudly at Loutt, "I do this for Camiss." There was proudful silence now, as the black fin swam past the patriarch.

Okent paused as he approached Camiss. He allowed Sprek to comfort her young one. She explained what was to be attempted. Sprek sang a soothing song for her offspring and clicked to Okent to begin.

The black fin approached Camiss very slowly. He could see the fear in her eyes. He knew she had heard stories of his kind hunting sperm whale pods. Okent could sense the pain she was in. The black fin chirped very softly. "I am Okent. I do NOT hunt your kind and I never will." The orca clicked a little louder and asked, "Will you trust me?"

Camiss had never seen an orca this close before. The elders in her pod would chase them away or do worse when they approached.

"My mother said you can remove the tooth-bone from my side." Okent clicked quietly. "Yes, I believe I can help with that."

Camiss spoke again, a little more bravely, "You helped the humpback years ago?"

Okent responded to her, "Yes, that is how we became friends, we have journeyed throughout the ocean together keeping each other safe."

Camiss asked, "Will it hurt?" Okent responded truthfully, "Yes, but I will be very gentle." Okent chirped, "Please watch your mother's and father's eye, and try not to laugh at my funny-looking white friend." The orca could see that young Camiss found humor in his remark about Hue. There was a slight smile in her eyes. The young sperm whale clicked, "I am ready."

Okent swam up to Camiss and caressed her with his enormous pectoral fin. The orca thought how small she was, how fragile. *I will help her, I will help the family. Then I will have words with Loutt.* The black fin moved along her body till he found the wound. The blood flow had stopped but would start again, once he removed the tooth-bone. This would be good to clean the wound but the blood might attract predators. Okent had a quick memory flash of dining on a shark's liver.

Okent thought, *That would be an ultimate reward*.

The orca studied the tooth-bone and determined where to bite. He would do his best to gently pull the object from the young female. Okent used the side of his mouth to grab the tooth-bone, and then turned his head away from Camiss's body. The tooth-bone resisted at first, but then slid out. The orca spat out the foul-tasting object. It sank to the bottom very quickly.

Camiss was delighted to be pain free. She let out a long ticking squeal to her parents that she felt much better. Okent began licking her wound to make sure, there were no pieces left inside.

The orca chirped, "All clear, you are set to go." The young female gleamed, "Much gratitude to you black fin."

The orca watched Camiss swim to her mother. She was much lighter in skin tone and was a smaller image of the large female sperm whale. The orca estimated her length at seventeen feet. She was the biggest newborn he had ever seen.

Okent turned to join up with Hue, but then right before him was Loutt. The orca stopped short and glared at the huge bull. The sperm whale was massive, just as Hue described. Two rows of conical teeth and a bulbous head over twenty feet in height. Okent remained very still. Loutt shifted his enormous head as to see the orca's eye. They stared at each other, neither one making any attempt to speak. Then suddenly, Loutt spoke in long clicks and low sounding chirps.

When he finished, he moved away from the orca. Loutt's body was so massive it created an underwater wave pushing the orca side to side. The great sperm whale quickly caught up to his mate and offspring. Then slowly they moved away and faded into the distant ocean. Sunlight reflected off their bodies making all three whales shimmer.

About this time Hue had joined up with Okent. They were both very quiet for while. The two companions were just thinking about the whole ordeal. The humpback and the orca continued breathing in the air of the salty sea and exhaling shortly after.

Hue spoke first. "Thank you, black fin, this was a good thing." Okent replied, "Yes, this was a good thing." There was more quietness between the orca and humpback.

The albino had to know, so he asked, "What did Loutt say to you?" The orca blew a string of bubbles and sank down, then answered Hue. "He said to me if I am ever in need of his assistance, please call out to him."

Hue asked how that could happen. Okent responded with a long low ticking click. The black fin had spoken a sperm whale's call for assistance. It meant Loutt would come, and he would bring others of his kind.

The albino clicked to the orca, "That is a very good thing."

CHAPTER TWENTY-FOUR
VESS BRINGS HOPE

The trusted elder scouts of Vess's pod had returned. They were gone only three sunsets. A young male orca was sent to fetch Herynn and bring her to Vess. The visiting matriarch responded immediately after being summoned and went to Vess's gathering, hoping for good news. "I have word, it is true that a large white humpback travels with an orca."

Herynn's heart jumped, then she chirped, "This could be my Okent." Vess continued, "My elder scouts have spoken to many other pods, and only four of them have seen or heard of these traveling companions." Vess then spoke to her elders, "Ask the pod for two volunteers to travel with our visiting matriarch. The journey will take her far from here. They must protect her from all dangers, especially the floating metal monsters from the surface."

Herynn asked, "Vess, please explain these floating metal monsters." "Yes, my dear friend. Very dangerous are these floating beasts. They kill all whales, and sometimes our kind as well."

Herynn listened intently. "How will I know this monster?" Vess thought for a moment, then answered. "They are noisy and there is always a terrible taste in the water about them. You will even taste death. Do not attempt to battle them but flee with haste."

The visiting matriarch bobbed her head up and down slowly, then she clicked, "I understand."

Vess spoke, "It is time for you to begin your search. You will be accompanied by two from my pod." Vess motioned to the volunteers to approach. "Both have requested this honor as you are special among our pod."

Herynn stayed respectful, still and patient awaiting the course direction. When Vess gave her the information, she said quick goodbyes to the pod, and moved away from the others, flanked by the two escorts. She would travel north up the coastline of South America for two days. Then meet up with the pod that saw the two companions. From there she would travel northwest and start her search. Herynn just knew she would find her lost offspring. This time there were too many clues not to succeed.

Hours passed for Herynn; she was in deep thought. The matriarch realized she had not even acknowledged her escorts. The female orca remembered meeting the younger orcas but was at a loss of their names. Herynn asked, "What are your names again?" Both escorts chirped and clicked their names together. She slowed to look at them both and figured she would ask one at a time. "Who are you?"

The female orca responded "Prinn." Herynn asked the male. "And you are?" The male chirped, "I am Trask."

"Do you plan on travelling with me for the entire journey?" Both orcas responded with, "Yes." Trask clicked, "We will be with you for as long as you are searching for your offspring."

Prinn chirped, "We are with you till you find Okent." Herynn responded, "I thank you both, the company is appreciated." All three orcas maintained a consistent speed. They were in sync with each other when they needed a breath. The mini pod would surface, breathe in, submerge, then surface and breathe out in perfect unison. Herynn knew it would be a few sunsets till she found Okent. *What will I say to him*, she thought. *Will he remember me after all these seasons?* The two escorts asked Herynn to speak louder. She did not realize she was clicking and chirping so quietly. "It was nothing, let us prepare to hunt."

A few moments later a school of tuna was detected, and the chase was on. All three orcas worked as a team and singled out a fish. The two escort orcas drove the lone tuna into the waiting mouth of Herynn. She swam over to share her catch.

Prinn chirped, "That was quick work for this mini pod." Trask clicked. The hunt continued four more times until all three orcas had full bellies.

Night had found its way to the mini pod. Herynn knew it would be best to rest and start again as the sun rose. She had dreams again of her offspring, but most of the dreams were about Okent.

The morning sun roused the mini pod. They determined a course and began to head north again. A few hours later they met up with the orca pod Vess had spoken of. There were friendly greetings and offers to share their food. Prinn and Trask accepted a freshly caught chinook and enjoyed a break from swimming. Herynn declined any food and was quick to gather the information needed to stay on course. She chirped to her escorts that it was time to depart. Herynn believed she would find Okent on this day. She chirped again loudly, "We are heading northwest."

CHAPTER TWENTY-FIVE
IS IT REALLY YOU?

Prinn was ahead of the mini pod by a few hundred yards out when she heard the strangest clicking and chirping followed by low ticking sounds. The young orca had come across a polite argument between two creatures. She recognized enough of the words that she could put together what was being discussed.

The conversation was about a horrible taste in the water and that they should be heading in an alternate direction. The two companions were at polite odds on what course to take. Then suddenly they stopped. There was complete silence. Only the sound of the underwater currents were audible.

Prinn paused and echolocated. Nothing... she thought *was I caught eavesdropping*? She clicked and listened, clicked and listened, but still nothing. The female orca began to turn and swim back to her mini pod. Suddenly there was a flash of black and white swimming past her. She was engulfed in a wave of underwater current. Prinn was spun around and turned upside down. "Wait!" she cried out. As she righted herself, she was confronted by Okent.

The orca swam right up to her and stared into her eye. "What do you want?" Okent asked. "Why are you following Hue and I?" Just then the great albino appeared behind Okent. When Prinn regained herself, she tried to answer, but was completely in awe at the size of Hue and that an orca was floating next to the humpback seemingly harmoniously.

Prinn chirped, "I mean no disrespect, I was intrigued by your conversation." Prinn paused then continued, "I recognized some of your words but other words I had never heard before."

Okent blew a few bubbles from his blowhole. "That is because some of the words are from the humpback language." The orca blew a few more bubbles then backed off from the young female orca. They both kept an eye on each other, trying to figure the other one out. Okent realized he had never been this close to an unrelated female orca before.

He became aware that he was staring at Prinn. He had noticed her size and shape, and the little black spots under her jaw. He liked the sound of her clicks and chirps and found them soothing somehow. The orca could taste the water around her. Okent had strange feelings running through his body. He thought, *what is happening to me? I should stop staring*. "Hue? HUE!?"

The albino approached slowly as to not startle the female orca. He introduced himself using orca clicks. Prinn was amazed that humpback could speak using orca words. She had no idea this was possible. Hue asked,

"What is your name my dear? Why are you here?" Prinn blurted her name nervously, and bubbles came out her blowhole this time, but not on purpose. Both orcas chirped a laugh at this and swam around each other. Hue called out "Black fin, why do you not introduce yourself to Prinn?" "Yes. I am Okent. Hello Prinn."

She clicked, "Hello Okent." Suddenly Prinn froze. She realized in that moment that this is Herynn's offspring. "Okent? You are Okent?! You are the offspring of Herynn!?" Okent pulled his body back and floated straight up looking at Prinn. "How do you know that? How can this be?" Prinn was chirping and clicking with great enthusiasm, "We have come to find you! She is here! We have traveled for twelve sunsets!" Prinn squealed, "It is you, Okent, we have found you!"

Hue heard every word and swam around the orcas, then stopped to speak. The humpback bellowed, "Black fin, answer her." As Okent looked away from Hue and turned back to Prinn, he saw his mother Herynn.

The black fin swam toward the approaching orca. Okent could see one large female orca being escorted by a smaller male. He heard the female click to the escort to stop swimming with her. She approached Okent with great wonderment in her eyes. "Is it really you, Okent?"

The orca slowly glided up to her and said, "I am Okent, are you… my mother?" "I am Herynn my water child."

The two orcas circled each other and caressed each other's fins. They both rose to the surface to slap the water with their tail flukes. Mother and son chirped and squealed to each other, talking over each other with great joy. Both began asking questions and shouting answers. After much talk and great leaps from the ocean both orcas rested at the surface and began to breathe in a quiet unison. "I have missed you, my son, I have dreamed about you. Somehow, I knew I would find you; I knew you were safe." Okent chirped, "I have been well, and safe." Herynn clicked again, "I heard the strangest tale that a lone orca was traveling with a white humpback."

Okent spoke, "This is true mother; his name is Hue. We have hunted together and kept each other safe for many seasons." Okent chirped with excitement. "Would you like to meet him?"

Herynn paused and looked upon her son, "Our kind and his kind do not associate well; I am not sure about this." Okent understood this to be true but explained, "Mother you can trust this friendship. It has grown over many seasons and many dangers. Together we have avoided the floating metal monsters."

Herynn knew of this beast from Vess. She asked, "You have seen the floating metal monster?"

Okent answered her, "Yes, Hue and I have seen the beasts and avoided them. They are a vile creature that hurt his kind."

Herynn thought for a few moments and then she chirped and clicked to Okent, "Yes, I will meet your travel companion."

Together they swam to Hue and Prinn. Herynn chirped to Trask and asked him to join the gathering. The young male escort thought to himself, *this should be interesting.* The albino swam to greet Okent and his newfound mother. He introduced himself and clicked to Herynn that he was honored to meet her. The matriarch returned his greeting with clicks and chirps. There was an uncomfortable tone in the clicks because this was very new to Herynn. She had never spoken to a humpback before.

Okent broke the awkwardness among the group with a breach and a deliberate splash. The orca then chirped "let us hunt together!"

Hue spoke, "I will remain here to feed. You four, be off! Good hunting." Then the albino turned away from the orcas and dove. They all watched the great humpback dive and level off. Hue's skin glowed ghostly white.

The mini pod watched him ascend with his mouth open, scooping hundreds of pounds of krill from the sea. When Hue surfaced, he ushered the sea water from his maw and swallowed his catch. The albino glanced at the four orcas and bellowed, "Be off with you, I wish to feed alone."

Okent knew this to be untrue; the albino always enjoyed company at mealtime. Hue wanted the orcas to socialize. It would be good for Okent to know his own kind. Prinn got the hint and chirped, "Shall we go?"

Then Okent darted away and at the same time chirped, "I am hungry for stingray." The rest of the mini pod followed his lead. Several stingrays were caught as well as squid and salmon. The hunt was more successful with four orcas working in unison to stalk prey. The night approached, and the orcas watched the sunset. Hue kept his distance, but was in communication with Okent as the day passed.

Through the night, many stories were told by Okent, of his ocean journeys. And Herynn spoke of her travels in search of her offspring. A few days had gone by and the mini pod knew it was time to leave the area. Okent and Prinn would spend time together when they could and were starting to become good friends. Herynn noticed and approved, but she also noticed that Trask had developed an interest in Prinn as well.

Chapter Twenty-Six
A Final Sunrise

McKeel was deep in thought. He could recall old times so well but was at a loss to remember yesterday. His appetite had weaned, and his entire body ached. The great humpback had viewed countless sunsets, countless sunrises and countless seasons. None of the young from his pod questioned his age anymore. McKeel knew the elders had asked all in the pod to cease this inquiry. Even if a member of the pod did ask, he could not answer the question with any certainty. McKeel always told the best stories and sang the most wonderful songs of all the humpbacks. Still, he knew his life was coming to an end. He would soon be with his creator. Perhaps he would visit the stars and travel next to the great object from his dreams. McKeel had heard its song only once, and would recreate the tones to the others. During this time, the pod would circle the great humpback and listen to him intently. Some of the humpbacks would float head down and enter a deep state of thought. It was a unique event and all would be grateful to McKeel for sharing his knowledge.

Babel approached McKeel slowly; she was not sure if he was slumbering on the surface. The female humpback watched her friend doze. She studied his body and viewed his many scars. There was a deep scar just past his mid-section, which had healed many seasons ago. McKeel had battled the floating metal monster and fended it off. None of the pod were harmed that day. She noticed his skin had lightened and many barnacles had formed along his head, body, and fins. Babel knew this crustacean growth slowed the great humpback down, adding to his fatigue. Her heart ached for her friend. She sensed his days were few. McKeel noticed Babel and invited her to join him. The two swam together and took in great breaths of air. There was an easy quiet between the two old friends. Both knew the inevitable would happen soon.

Babel rubbed her pectoral fin against McKeel's. She began singing to the great humpback. Her song soothed the old and wise patriarch. He sang back to her. The longtime companions began to speak of adventures they shared and the future of the pod. McKeel brought up Okent first. The great humpback expressed his affections for the orca, and his hopes that he had survived.

The elder female looked McKeel in the eye and said, "I have heard stories of a lone orca."

McKeel seemed to brighten up a bit. He was curious as to what Babel meant. "Please tell me what you know."

The female humpback continued, "I have heard from other pod elders that a single orca travels with a white humpback. I had always hoped it was Okent, and that he had found his way in the ocean."

McKeel clicked with great joy, "I believe this to be true Babel. It would make sense, two different creatures with similar struggles banding together to survive. Yes, it could be just that." McKeel floated to the ocean surface and took a deep breath of salty air. "I will miss this world, but not as much as I have missed Okent."

Babel asked if she could spend the day with the great humpback. She clicked, "Please tell me some of your stories before you met me."

McKeel rolled over and did a shallow dive. He turned his massive body around to look the female humpback in the eye. "Where should I begin?"

Babel answered, "Tell me of your father and mother. Tell me of your first mate." She already knew the stories, as McKeel had talked of his family many times. But Babel knew it would help comfort the great humpback to talk of his youth.

The afternoon had come, and the pair began feeding. Babel noticed that McKeel only took a few mouthfuls of krill. But she kept her concerns to herself. This could be her last time alone with this great patriarch, and she wanted to relish in the moment as long as possible.

Suddenly a younger female approached the two older humpbacks with great speed and panic in her clicks and chirps. "The pod is being attacked!"

The three humpbacks turned and quickly headed back toward the pods location. All three took turns popping an eye above the water to gain sight of the other humpbacks. A short distance away, a black cloud floated toward them from the horizon. All three humpbacks were assaulted by a horrible taste in the water. There was floating debris, blood, and the taste of death. Several dolphins swam past the humpbacks with great momentum, and terror-filled eyes as they fled away from the black smoke.

Sounds of panic and fear were heard by all three humpbacks. McKeel increased his pace and was the first of them to see the horrid beast. There, among the pod, was the floating metal monster. The cruel creature had managed to stick a tooth-bone into a young male humpback. Blood dispersed in the water around the dying whale. The floating metal monster was pulling the humpback to its side. Upright walking mammals readied themselves with longer tooth-bones and began cutting the young whale. Clicks and squeals of great agony could be heard coming from the humpback. Then all the pod felt the young humpback's heart stop beating. There was no time to understand what was happening as all were in a full panic. Clicks and high-pitched chirps asking what to do engulfed the pod. Only McKeel answered, he ordered everyone to leave the area in different directions. "SWIM!" "FAST!" "NOW!"

The great humpback turned to fight the beast. He spied the floating metal monster turning toward a lone humpback. McKeel recognized the coloring and shape of the female humpback's body. The patriarch pumped his enormous tail flukes with tremendous power. He began clicking to Babel as loud as he could. McKeel bellowed to swim away, to dive, to change her course. He was almost upon the monster when he saw Babel do a deep dive. A tooth-bone entered the water just above the female humpback's dorsal area. It missed her side by a few feet. The great humpback continued toward the floating metal monster and rammed into the beast's side. The monster listed hard to the opposite side of the strike. McKeel heard its moans of anger and the whishing noise ceased.

Pain ran through the great humpback's jaw and skull. All that mattered to him was that Babel was safe. McKeel did a fast dive and clicked to the female humpback. She responded, "I am safe!" He moved to find her and then meet up with rest of the scattered humpback pod.

McKeel felt an explosion of agony on his right side. Then a second explosion of pain registered. The great humpback turned to find the source. He could not see what had happened to his body, but he did see great amounts of blood floating by his eye. He bellowed in horrible pain. Babel rushed to his side. She could see very long tooth-bones protruding from McKeel's mid-section. Great openings in his skin were allowing tremendous amounts of blood to flow into the sea. The ocean waves had begun to turn crimson. The female humpback clicked and chirped to dive, swim away, go deep.

Babel bellowed to McKeel, "Save yourself!"

CHAPTER TWENTY-SEVEN
THE OCEAN IS BROKEN

H ue was the first to hear it. Life in the ocean was crying out in fear and horror. The albino knew something was wrong. He called to the group and asked them to listen. Screams could be heard from a few miles away. The mini pod heard cries of confusion and terror. Hue bellowed loudly, "The ocean is broken! Follow me, I will need everyone's help."

Without question everyone joined in Hue's pursuit. Herynn fell in alongside the albino, Trask followed her, and Prinn and Okent took up the rear. The great albino began to pick up speed and the rest of the mini pod started to hear terrifying clicks and chirps. Among the many cries of fear, Okent thought he heard a familiar voice. Then he recognized two voices from his past. The orca realized it was Babel calling out in anguish.

"Please save yourself, please." Then Okent heard a second voice, clicking to stay away, to flee from here. The orca recognized the clicking and chirps, they were coming from….. McKeel! He could tell the great humpback had been wounded and was in tremendous pain.

Okent pumped his tail flukes with all his strength. He passed the group in a black and white blur. Hue called after him to slow his approach, "black fin! be cautious, I believe it is a floating metal monster attack."

The orca ignored his friend and increased his speed. He was rushing to his adoptive mother and mentor. Okent leaped from the ocean to catch a surface view. Hue was correct; there was an enormous floating metal monster on the surface. But it was tilted slightly down, as if the beast were sinking. There were upright walking mammals moving around its top area. The taste in the water was of blood and death.

The orca came across Babel first, but they did not have time to respond to each other. Okent could see his old mentor being pulled sideways toward the floating metal monster. The great humpback was crying out with clicks to leave him, and to save yourselves.

"This is what I want; save the pod!" Okent rushed to his old mentor. McKeel could feel his body grow numb; the pain was turning into a piercing throb. The great humpback said to himself, *it will all be over soon.* The old patriarch felt the pull of the lines on his skin, he applied no resistance to the tugging motion. McKeel's mind was begging his creator for the release of his life. *Take me, my creator, now.*

Then there was a blur of black and white before McKeel's left eye, and an underwater wave of great force washed over him. The great humpback sensed his body was no longer moving. There was a new sensation of a dull pain being sent to his brain. McKeel could feel the great tooth-bones being broken into pieces, bit by bit. Then there was a sudden release of pain as the tips were pulled from his body. The great whale could now feel himself sinking, spinning down, heading away from the surface. McKeel could hear all kinds of chatter, clicks and chirps. He could barely make out the words but knew he was somehow being moved away from the floating metal monster. The humpback's lungs ached for air, and at that moment several other whales began helping the orca push on his underside and lower jaw. McKeel was being raised to the surface. He took a deep breath as his blowhole cleared the ocean water. The great humpback watched the blur of black and white swim past his eye again. There was a familiar presence to the creature. He wondered if the young orca had grown and returned to the pod. Could it be? McKeel could not think clearly. He rolled to his side and moved his eye to the surface of the water.

The old patriarch could see a great battle was being fought in the distance. There were four orcas charging the floating mental monster and leading it away. The distraction allowed Babel and three other humpbacks to push him elsewhere. McKeel floated on the surface with the help of other returning humpbacks from his pod. The great whale fell unconscious. McKeel's pod gathered around him, and the largest elders swam in a circle of protection around them. They knew that, with this much blood floating in the water, there was the possibility that the death fish would come searching for the source.

Okent was the first of the orcas to join up with the humpback pod. Many whales recognized him, and some were pleased that he had survived. Others still resented him but the orca did not care. He swam to his dying mentor's side. Herynn, Prinn, and Trask thought it best to keep a distance from the humpback pod. The matriarch watched her offspring nuzzle up to the great humpback. She heard Okent cry out a long high squeal. McKeel sang to the orca and then clicked "This is the way of the ocean. I am ready for my life to end." The orca rubbed his head against

McKeel's great pectoral fin. He then gently pushed his head under the fin. Okent could hear the great humpbacks heart, pumping slower and slower. McKeel looked into Okent's eye and said "I have never stopped thinking of you… my son."

The entire pod and the orcas all heard the breath leave McKeel's body. There was a slow and quiet wooosh of air, and then no further sounds came from the old whale. After a few moments, the great humpback slipped under the ocean surface and began to sink. All the humpback whales watched their patriarch float downward. McKeel's body was so massive it created a slight suction behind it. The smaller humpbacks had to adjust their positions to stay near the surface. Many chanted, "This is the way of the sea, this is the way of the sea, this is the way of the sea."

Okent floated down alongside his friend for as long as his lungs could hold air. Then he clicked a quiet goodbye to his mentor, his protector, his father. The orca watched the humpback sink deeper and deeper into the ocean abyss. Okent's vision was being hampered by the growing darkness. Sunlight could only penetrate so far down. The orca's body began to remind him it was time to breathe. Just as Okent was moving out of his hovering stance he saw blue sharks following the descending whale. Black tip and white tip sharks began circling McKeel's body as well, following the trail of blood. This was the first whale fall Okent had ever witnessed, and his heart ached. He then clicked a quiet thank you to his mentor and turned away.

The orca rose to the surface and floated there for a short while, collecting his thoughts. Then he swam to join the humpbacks and greet his adoptive mother Babel. Okent thought it would be best to introduce Herynn, Prinn, and Trask to her right away. She was now the head matriarch of the pod. He would ask her to welcome the other orcas for a short time. Okent wanted to get to know Herynn better and make amends with Babel for the way he left the humpback pod. The orca was exhausted and asked everyone to stay in their own pods for the night.

"We can grieve our loss of McKeel and keep a watch for the return of the floating metal monster." Many humpbacks kept a distance from the orcas as there was little trust, but an uncomfortable peace between the species would last through the evening.

Hue went to the mini orca pod and thanked them for their assistance while the humpbacks tried to help McKeel. "Let us talk more at sunrise, I have a plan of revenge," He said before returning to the humpbacks.

Okent woke from the sounds of both pods speaking amongst themselves. He went to find Babel but stopped a short distance away. He floated to the surface to catch a breath of air and waited.

She was in a deep discussion with Hue. Both whales were speaking of McKeel's death and the cause of it. The albino told Babel that the black fin talked so much about McKeel that he felt he had known him already. Hue expressed great sorrow in not ever having a conversation with the pod's patriarch. Babel told Hue that the great humpback would have welcomed him into his pod. This was good to hear as Hue missed his own pod from time to time. Over the years, and more than once, the albino would sometimes hear songs from members of his family miles away, but always kept to himself. Hue wanted Babel to know that the black fin kept him company on their long travels and he enjoyed their friendship. The albino asked her if she would like to hear of his adventures with Okent sometime. Babel was somewhat flattered that Hue wanted to spend time together. She accepted his offer, clicking, "Yes, thank you." The two humpbacks continued discussing McKeel and the pod's next course of action. Hue spoke of his plan to rid the ocean of the metal beast.

The conversation ended when Okent approached the two humpbacks. Hue greeted Okent then took his leave. The orca knew the albino very well after all these seasons together. Okent was aware of Hue's anger and a bubble stream would not comfort his old friend today.

The orca touched pectoral fins with his adoptive mother and they spoke for many hours.

Chapter Twenty-Eight
THE BEGINNING OF THE END

"**N**o more, never again, we end this forever!" Hue bellowed. "We will end the life of this monster. It has invaded our ocean world, and it takes our family and friends away, never to be seen again." Hue bellowed again. "No more, now we fight." All the humpbacks gathered in a circle to listen to the albino's plan. When Hue had explained what should be done, the others clicked in approval. "The strongest swimmers of the pod will initiate the attack. We will create chaos for the floating metal monster! Then the largest of the elders will attack from below and crush its belly!"

Many humpbacks flapped their flukes on the water's surface. Songs were being sung and sent out into the ocean to bring more humpbacks to join the campaign. Hue continued, "The young and newborns will stay with their aunties and move a great distance away from this battle." More clicks were spoken amongst the pod to express approval.

Hue called to Okent, "You, my friend, shall stay behind and swim a perimeter around the younger humpbacks, you will keep them away from the floating metal monster."

The orca squealed, "I will not do that! I will assist in the battle, and so will the other orcas."

Hue paused then swam close to Okent's right eye. "No, my friend, you are fast on the water and faster under it but the humpbacks have the strength."

The black fin was growing angry; he spoke to Hue with loud clicks and chirps: "They killed my mentor; I want to be part of this metal monster's destruction."

Hue spoke over the orca's rant, "I will need you to protect the young and the newborns if this does not end well for the elder humpbacks."

Okent knew the albino's logic was sound and his plan was meticulously thought out. This was the best way to protect the pod. The orca then agreed with his friend using a very soft clicking tone.

Hue spoke again, in a more passive clicking tone as well. "Black fin, I wish to talk to you of family, I wish you to start your own pod." Okent began to protest but was cut off by the albino immediately. "Do not interrupt me again black fin." Hue paused a moment then clicked, "Herynn has spoken to me of Prinn, and we both agree she would make a good mate for you. Okent, go to Prinn now and tell her of your feelings."

The orca was at a loss for words. He had many questions spinning through his brain. *How did Hue know? How did Herynn know? Can others tell?* Then the orca chirped to Hue. "How will I know what to say to her? What if there is no return of…"

Just then Hue whacked the side of Okent's torso with his pectoral fin. "My oblivious friend, just look at the way she acts around you! Look at how she stares at you from wherever she is."

Hue bellowed, "NOW GO! Find her, black fin, before Trask asks her to be his mate." Hue chirped sarcastically, "Or have you not noticed how he watches her?"

Okent darted away, his mind racing. He was full of love for Prinn, and at the same time his heart was breaking over the death of McKeel. The last few sunsets had been eventful. Finding both of his mothers, meeting Prinn and losing his mentor. Okent's heart was full of emotion and anger. As he swam to the orca mini pod, he realized the importance of the request Hue had bestowed upon him. To protect the newborns and young was a great honor. It was only asked of the bravest amongst the pod. Okent would ask the other orcas to assist him. Together, the mini pod of orcas would protect Babel's pod.

Chapter Twenty-Nine
NOW THERE ARE TWO

An elder scout was sent to find the floating metal monster. After a few hours he returned with news. He approached Hue, Babel, and the rest of the elders, all gathered in a semi-circle. The matriarch spoke up when she saw the scout returning: "What can you tell us Niv?" "I have disturbing information."

Hue clicked "Tell us what you have learned." The humpback did not pause; he came right out with what he observed, and it was not good. "There are now two floating metal monsters."

There was a flurry of chirps and clicks, even low toned bellows exclaiming "NO!" Babel asked, "What else, Niv?"

He clicked to the humpback pod with fear in his tone. "The second monster is much larger than the first. It appears to be assisting the wounded metal monster. It does not list to the side any longer."

Okent had been listening to the conversation and asked to speak. Hue looked to Babel for permission, and she nodded yes. The albino clicked, "Tell us your thoughts black fin."

Okent said, "This changes nothing. In a short time, several other humpback pods will join us, we will charge the horrid beasts, and sink them." There were chirps and clicks from the elders, who all agreed, this changes nothing.

Hue bellowed "We will wait for the arrival of the other pods and expand on our existing plan of attack. This will be our final battle with the floating metal monster. No longer will they slash us with their tooth-bone sticks." Hue bellowed again, "No more blood of whales will be spilled into the sea!"

A short time later other humpbacks could be heard approaching. There were many songs being sung in unison. Conversation of cooperation and bravery came from the arriving humpbacks. Introductions were made and familiar faces were recognized. All were told of the orca pod, and that their function was not to be interfered with in any way.

Babel began by greeting all the humpbacks who joined her pod. "Welcome and thank you for assisting in this battle. Many of your family members have been lost to the floating metal monster. I say, no more, and on this day we make the beast regret the murders of our pod members." The matriarch clicked again, "I ask you to listen to a member of my pod, and his plan to stop the monsters forever."

Hue approached the pod from Babel's right side. It was becoming noticeable how much time the two spent together these days. This was a good match, and many thought so, but still, it would have to wait. The albino began discussing his plan and dividing up the pod. There would be many diversions and only a few of the largest elders would actually attack the metal monster. A course was set and each grouping of humpbacks went their separate directions.

Hue was the last to move away from the gathering point. He looked toward Okent. The orca was watching him and had listened to all of Hue's strategic plans. The albino clicked to the orca, "Protect the aunts and newborns with all your strength."

Okent responded with a bubble stream. Then clicked, "This is for McKeel."

CHAPTER THIRTY
A BLACK FIN'S REVENGE

The humpbacks began moving in different directions. They were all following Hue's plan of attack and proceeded with great determination. Today was the last day on the ocean for these two floating metal monsters. Babel watched her pod members join with other humpbacks from different pods. Hue flanked his group and heard clicks from other elders that the beasts had been sighted. Okent remained behind to protect the newborns and aunties. He felt a great responsibility in doing so. Herynn, Prinn, and Trask all swam a perimeter around the young humpbacks. There were a few nursing mothers in the group as well. Okent was grateful for this because the mothers would add much needed comfort to the young. The ocean was charged with tension and excitement. The young humpbacks could sense something dangerous was about to happen. All four orcas were on high alert. Their echolocation abilities would be put to good use today. This was an excellent way to monitor the area and the young whales. Okent would protect both of his families at all costs. The orca managed a quick body count of the young and their mothers. There were four newborns and seven young humpbacks. He counted eleven nursing mothers and four aunties. He thought of Hue and his promise to keep them all safe. He thought of McKeel as well. Okent had done a body count of all the attacking humpbacks. There were twenty-seven humpbacks that would be used as a distraction and bait. The orca had counted nine attacking elders. They were the biggest humpbacks Okent had ever seen. Some were bigger than Hue and some were even approaching McKeel's size. The orca thought to himself, *the floating beasts will die today.* He clicked to Hue, "No more!"

The humpbacks approached the floating metal monsters to make themselves visible while the largest elders dove deep under the beasts. Within moments the bait was taken. Both floating beasts coughed black smoke from their blowholes and lurched forward towards the pod of humpbacks. Clicks and chirps went out to stay fast and strong. "Be brave" was sung over and over. As the beasts approached the newly formed pod, the humpbacks began slapping the water surface and diving. This caused the beasts to split in two different directions. Divide and conquer was Hue's plan all along. The humpbacks all began circling and diving under the beasts. The whales were causing confusion and chaos, as the albino predicted.

Tooth-bone after tooth-bone missed their targets. Sometimes the tooth-bones almost struck their marks. Many clicks were sent out to "be careful, and be cautious." It was more important to distract the ocean intruders.

Babel continued to monitor the battle around the floating metal monsters. She noticed a few times the tooth-bones came too close to one of her pod members. She clicked to Hue, "Order them to remain underwater longer, and always come up in a different section of ocean."

The albino concurred and clicked the order. He could see the metal beasts growing frustrated; they were whipping around the surface and listing back and forth. The humpbacks had created huge wave's, and the beasts were not responding well to the turmoil. Hue knew the time was right and sent out orders to the distracting humpbacks to dive deep. Now it was the elders' turn.

The largest of the elder humpbacks had gathered under the metal beasts. One by one they would strike the bellies of the floating monsters. Each elder humpback gathered tremendous momentum and smashed into the bottom side of the beast. There was a great clanging ring and the metal beasts moaned at each strike. Great cracks formed along the underside of the smaller monster. The whining whirling noise stopped, and the beast began to sink. No more black smoke came from the monster's top. Many upright walking mammals jumped into the ocean. With all this movement in the ocean and the smell of blood in the water the humpbacks knew the death fish would come and take the upright mammals away. Hue clicked and chirped to Okent that the beast that killed McKeel was sinking to the bottom of the ocean. Many upright walking mammals were also sinking. Hue bellowed, "You have your revenge black fin."

The elders began their attack on the larger floating metal monster. This beast had not one but two slashing teeth spinning on its underside. This area was to be avoided. One of the elders brushed up against the spinning teeth on the smaller beast and was cut. Blood had seeped out of the wound and the elder retreated, clicking a warning to stay away from the slashing teeth.

The largest elder attacked first and barely inflicted any damage to the floating metal monster's belly. Then another humpback elder rammed the same area and still nothing happened to the beast. Confusion struck all the attacking elders. Hue heard the clicks and bellowed to retreat and regroup.

The floating metal monster began to circle the elder humpbacks as if preparing to attack back. Then suddenly several tooth-bones entered the ocean at once. Two elders were struck, and Hue ordered them to dive quickly. But it was no use; both humpbacks' were now being dragged toward the beast. The whales that acted as a distraction all became aware of their fellow humpbacks injuries and cried out to help them.

The remaining elders continued to smash into the floating metal monster. But nothing could stop it; the beast coughed more black smoke and pulled the two wounded humpbacks closer to its side. Niv had watched the upright mammals climb out of the ocean and onto the beast's back. He reported this sighting to Babel immediately. She clicked the information to Hue and sent orders to end the attack. The larger floating metal monster was too strong. The albino bellowed to the humpback matriarch to send for Okent quickly. "We can save our wounded friends!" Babel remembered hearing from Hue the orca's ability to free whales from the tooth-bone stick. She ordered Niv to find Okent and send him to Hue immediately.

The younger humpback quickly found Okent and told him of Babel's commands. Okent understood and in a blur was on his way to the albino. The orca found Hue and was made aware of the injured elders. Hue bellowed, "Black fin, save them!"

The orca swam with all his might toward the two injured humpbacks. Okent quickly found the tooth-bone imbedded on the right side of the first elder. He went right to work chewing at the horrid tooth. The elder was larger than Hue and was providing great resistance to the pulling motion of the line attached to the stick.

Okent bit right through the line; it made a snap sound and bounced across the ocean surface. Next, he gently twisted the tooth out of the great humpback like he did a few seasons ago for Camiss. The orca had a flash of memory of Loutt. *"Call me and I will come with others."* Okent spat the tooth-bone out and swam to the next elder in a black and white swirl.

He found the humpback against the side of the floating metal monster. The orca watched long tooth-bone sticks being pushed into the elder and great pieces of flesh were being taken off the humpback. There was a tremendous amount of blood in the water and the taste of death was everywhere. Okent realized that it was too late for this elder humpback. The whale had given its life to fight the floating metal beast.

Hue bellowed and clicked for the orca to respond, "Black fin? Black fin, tell me your location. BLACK FIN!"

Okent was in a daze at what had just happened in front of him. He watched a second humpback die in as many days. The orca could still hear the albino's cry in his head. *"No more, never again!"*

Hue bellowed again, and this time others joined in, "Black fin, find us!" Okent's thoughts released him, and he returned to reality. He chirped to Hue that he was unharmed and that he will return shortly. Then he paused to gather his thoughts. Okent always thought before he spoke.

"One elder is safe and returning to the pod, the second elder has been taken by the metal monster." Hue clicked, "I understand. Please return to the pod." Okent agreed but chirped and clicked, "I need a moment first; I have an idea."

The orca inhaled the largest breath he could and dove very deep; Deeper than he had ever gone before. When he felt it was the right depth, he stopped. Okent remembered how the words were pronounced, he remembered the tone used, and he remembered the exact way to sing. He thought, *this has to work.*

The orca called out in his loudest voice, "Help me Loutt."

CHAPTER THIRTY-ONE
THE RETURN OF LOUTT

The orca stared into the abyss that was the ocean. He cried out two more times for Loutt's assistance. Just before his fourth attempt Okent heard a response. The tone that was bellowed back was the loudest he had ever heard or felt. "I am Loutt, I am coming to you black fin." The orca felt his lungs ache, but he could not move. Then in the watery distance a shape appeared. The size of the newly formed body was immense. Okent could tell from this distance that Loutt was even larger than before. The orca also realized that the great sperm whale was being accompanied by two other sperm whales. He could actually, feel the water being pushed toward him from the approaching whales forward momentum. The orca dashed to the surface to fill his lungs with air. He returned to find Loutt and his two companions waiting for him. The great sperm whale spoke first, "It is good to see you alive black fin. This is Sprek's brother Cach, and this is Phi. What say you black fin?!"

Okent's ears were ringing at the volume the great sperm whale used to click his words. The orca was amazed at how large these whales were and just stared at them. Okent thought of blowing a bubble stream but decided against doing so. He chose his words carefully. The orca began to click and chirp, "Loutt, I request your assistance. I and many other humpbacks are in a battle with the floating metal monsters from the surface. We have decided that no more humpbacks will be taken away by them."

Loutt interrupted, "Black fin, you have joined in battle against these floating beasts? They do not hunt your kind, only my kind! Explain this choice!"

Okent continued, "I watched them kill my mentor and I have watched them take another humpbacks life. Hue has devised a plan to remove them from the ocean." Okent chirped loudly, "We have killed one already, but the second beast is too big and too strong; it continues to hunt humpbacks." Okent asked, "Can you assist in our battle?"

Loutt swam to Okent, so they were now eye to eye. The great sperm whale quietly clicked to the orca, "I do this for Camiss." Okent knew exactly what Loutt meant and blew a stream of bubbles from his blowhole. The orca turned away quickly and chirped and clicked to the three great sperm whales to follow him.

"This way to the battle!" All three sperm whales caught up to Okent in a few strokes of their tails. Cach noticed the water had a horrible taste to it and the taste of death was about. Phi clicked in agreement and then asked, "What is the plan Loutt?"

The great sperm whale bellowed three words to his companions, "Smash the beast!"

CHAPTER THIRTY-TWO
THE FINAL BATTLE

O kent clicked and chirped to Hue, "Tell me your position, I bring Loutt, and two more to assist us. They will fight the floating metal beasts!" The albino bellowed an approval for all to hear. The white humpback told the pods to reposition themselves as before and begin to distract the beast.

"There is a new plan of attack my fellow humpbacks," Hue clicked very loudly to the pod, "Now we have the advantage of size!"

The orca was in visual range of Hue and the humpback pods. He clicked to the albino their position. Okent could hear and see the pods tormenting the floating metal monster. The whales would breach and submerge over and over. The beast continued to shoot its tooth-bone sticks at the humpbacks.

Black smoke belched from its blowhole, and there was a slick gooey substance floating about the body of the monster. The whooshing noise grew more intense as the beast struggled to turn. It was surrounded by over thirty humpback whales now. Hue clicked over and over to be cautious, submerge quickly, always alter your course, swim very fast. The pod complied and the distraction was working. Confusion engulfed the horrid beast. The orca knew the floating metal monster and the upright walking mammals would soon be gone from the ocean.

Okent clicked to Hue again, "We are in position, and we are awaiting your call to attack. What say you, old friend?"

The albino responded with a loud bellow to hold fast. "We must wait for the perfect moment," Hue clicked, "Hold...hold..." The beast was almost in position. "Black fin get ready!" Hue bellowed the loudest cry he could, NOW...!" Okent clicked to Loutt, Cach and Phi, "ATTACK!"

At the same time, Hue clicked to all the pods to retreat, dive deep, and swim fast. Within mere moments the humpbacks had vanished from the sea. The floating beast turned in circles. It had exhausted its supply of tooth-bone sticks and was about to head away from the circling whales.

Great globs of black smoke came from its blowhole and the whining increased along with the whooshing noise. Hue could tell the beast was frightened and heading away from the distracting pods but it was too late.

The humpbacks had moved away with great speed. The area was cleared for the sperm whales attack. All the humpbacks remained under water and at a distance but could still see what was about to happen. Then, in an instant, all three sperm whales were upon the floating metal monster.

Cach and Phi began their run, on opposite sides of the beast. They would smash the monster and crush its body just below the ocean surface. Loutt moved under the beast and would come at its belly. The two sperm whales on either side rammed the beast with incredible force. Both Cach and Phi weighed in at eighty-five thousand pounds each. They both swam their top speed to gain momentum. This cracked and crushed the sides of the metal monster. There was an incredible squealing noise as its sides concaved in. The humpback pods heard this agonizing sound and knew what it meant. They cheered with chirps and clicks. The floating beast was wounded and vulnerable. The black smoke stopped coming from its blowhole and the whooshing noise ceased. The beast had stopped moving and great amounts of the ocean were spilling into the openings of the monsters sides.

Loutt was observing the event from forty feet below. The great sperm whale watched the beast shudder and stall. He calculated his ascent and would bring his ninety-thousand pounds to full speed. First, he dove down another hundred feet and then rose from the ocean depths in a perfect ascending arch. Loutt struck the belly of the floating monster with tremendous force. There was a sound of metal cracking and a ringing sound bounced outward through the sea. The beast imploded in on itself and began to sink. Several walking upright mammals leaped into the ocean, screaming in terror and confusion. A call to the death fish rang out from the dying monster.

All three sperm whales gathered together and watched the beast sink into the dark abyss of the sea. Perhaps it would provide a meal to life on the bottom or maybe just rot on the ocean floor. The taste of blood and death followed it downward. Either way, the whales did not care. They turned from the sinking beast and rose to the surface. Loutt clicked to the other two sperm whales,

"This floating metal monster would never be seen or heard from again."

CHAPTER THIRTY-THREE
MY BEST FRIEND IS OKENT

Loutt noticed the arrival of all the humpbacks. They circled the great sperm whales and began clicking and singing them praise and many thanks to the beast killers. Loutt, Cach, and Phi were grateful and said so, but all three had headaches which they kept to themselves. Giant squid would be their reward meal this day.

Hue approached the sperm whales and clicked to Loutt, "How is Camiss? and what of Sprek?"

The great sperm whale bellowed, "They are well, but now I must return to them." The albino understood and watched the three sperm whales begin to depart. Just then Okent approached, and chirped to Loutt, "Please give my regards to Camiss and Sprek." Loutt bellowed, "I will black fin, and fare thee well."

The orca watched the three sperm whales surface and take in a huge breath of ocean air, then submerge and turn away from the humpback pod. The destroyers of the floating metal monster faded into the ocean. The orca remembered watching three sperm whales fade in a similar way a few seasons before and chirped a quiet "goodbye."

Hue swam to Okent's side. The two companions floated near the surface and remained silent. Then Hue clicked, "It is over, the ocean will be safer for all humpbacks and all whales."

The orca blew a bubble stream from his blowhole and chirped to Hue, "Shall we go my friend?" The albino asked, "Where to black fin?" Okent responded "To continue our ocean journey."

The humpback clicked, "Okent, I have always told you the truth, I wish to remain with Babel and the other humpbacks. She has asked me to be her mate, and I accepted." The orca was both delighted and surprised, and it showed in his eyes. Hue bellowed, "Speak your thoughts black fin!" Okent paused a bit then chirped to Hue, "I have never heard you call me Okent before.

The albino looked into the orca's eye and said, "Okent is the name of my best friend, and you, black fin are my best friend." The two companions continued to float on the surface and began to breathe in unison. The orca and the albino touched pectoral fins for a short amount of time, then they returned to their respective pods.

The rest of the humpbacks remained together for a short while saying their goodbyes, and then parted ways. Babel swam to Hue and asked, "Are you ready to swim northeast?" Hue clicked a warm "Yes."

The matriarch then turned to her adopted son and asked, "Okent, have you asked Prinn to be your mate? I think she will answer yes." The orca swam to Babel's side and nuzzled her like he did when he was just a newborn.

"I will ask her mother, and thank you for all you have done for me; may I visit you sometime?"

Babel embraced Okent with her pectoral fin and chirped, "I hope you do; and maybe then you will introduce me to your newborn." The orca squealed a warm goodbye and said, "I will return mother."

Hue and Babel watched Okent join the mini orca pod. Herynn chirped a thank you to Hue. Then orca matriarch looked at Babel and chirped and clicked to her, in a way only a mother would understand. Herynn expressed great amounts of gratitude for caring for her newborn. She then turned away and began to swim southeast. Trask joined her side and expressed the need to hunt. He clicked, "Maybe chinook would be our prey this evening." Herynn agreed with a quick chirp, "agreed."

Okent swam to Prinn and asked her to be his mate. Her answer came quickly and Okent sensed she had been waiting very patiently for this moment. The newly mated pair caressed each other's pectoral fins and watched the humpbacks fade into the ocean. Light danced off all their backs, making their skin shimmer and glow. The two orcas then turned and swam together near the surface. They took in a breath, submerged, and quickly caught up to the Herynn's mini pod. Then Okent heard a bellow from Hue, "Farewell black fin, farewell."

The orca responded in kind, "And you too my friend, you too."

CHAPTER THIRTY-FOUR
A NEW SEASON

The mini pod remained to together for several weeks. The four orcas had joined up with several others that were separated from their pod during a storm. The mini pod had doubled. There were two younger orcas amongst the four. They all remained together for companionship, safety, and to hunt.

Herynn began speaking of returning to her pod. She had been away for too long and knew Joop and Joom would be wondering if she ever found Okent. The eight orcas had gathered just before sunset and discussed their options. Trask expressed his desire to return to Vess's pod. He would tell her that Herynn had found her offspring and of the great battle he participated in. Then Trask looked at Okent and chirped, "I will also tell Vess that Prinn is safe and will not be returning to her pod; I will tell the grand matriarch that Prinn is Okent's mate now."

There was a pause of chirps and clicks between the orcas. Trask had stated what everyone was thinking. Okent swam close to Trask's eye and chirped, "Thank you my friend, I am glad to know you."

That night the orcas slumbered together for the last time. In the morning Trask would set out to find Vess's pod, which he knew to be off the Central American coast this time of year. Fortunately, the four orcas that joined the mini pod were heading south and Trask would travel in safety. It would be an ten-sunset journey. Trask clicked, "I will be fine; we will depart at sunrise."

Herynn was the first to stir as the morning light filled the sky. She plotted a course using the sun and sensing the earth's magnetic circumference. The matriarch could also tell by the season where her pod would most likely be in the coming weeks. There was a short farewell from the orcas to each other. They moved in opposite directions and fell into the rhythm of the waves.

Okent and his mother swam together and continued to get to know each other. She told him of the pod he would be joining. The matriarch spoke of Joom and Joop, his older brothers. "They were left in charge while I searched for you."

Okent chirped, "I do not remember them mother." Herynn told the story of their bravery and how they protected her while she hid him away. With enthusiasm Okent chirped, "I look forward to meeting my brothers."

The matriarch continued, "By this time I imagine they have chosen mates and wish to start their own pod." Okent remained quiet. "What is it my son?" The orca answered his mother, "Prinn and I have good news."

Herynn clicked, "Okent, I am aware." There was a squeal of joy from all three orcas as they moved in sync, breathing together in time with the waves of the sea.

CHAPTER THIRTY-FIVE
THE LITTLE ONE

A season and a half had passed for Okent and his mate Prinn. He accompanied her into a shallow cove on a warm autumn night. There were large clumps of seaweed and kelp floating close to the shoreline. The moon was very bright and reflected off the water's surface. The ocean was smooth and quiet. The two orcas were alone, but the pod remained close by. This night was very special to the mated pair as Prinn's first calf was about to enter the ocean world. She was very proud to give Okent a water child. The pain in her abdomen came in pulses, increasing as she swam in a circle. Prinn stayed close to the surface, and she tried to control her breathing. Okent chirped comforting tones to her and caressed her body as he swam with her.

Then it happened, a little one emerged. First, the tail flukes, and a puff of blood, followed by a torso, pectoral fins, and a small dorsal fin folded over. Finally, a small head with a mouth full of teeth and a blowhole eager to take its first breath. Okent and Prinn brought their newborn to the surface and watched her do just that. They noticed right away that their newborn was very healthy and very white. She was so white she shimmered in the moonlight. She was glowing the way Hue would under water.

Okent chirped to the pod that he had a daughter; "Prinn and the newborn are doing just fine, we will return to the pod sometime soon."

Prinn swam very close to Okent, and they watched their little one swim just a few feet ahead of them. She was a few minutes old and already becoming a matriarch. The three orcas swam together and breathed in the night air. Prinn clicked, "What is her name Okent?" The orca looked at his little one with all the love a father could have for his offspring.

"We will call her Luna."

THANKS FOR THE READ!

This is my first book. I began writing it in the spring of 2023. It was a labor of great joy and very challenging, as it was my first attempt at being an author. The concept for the story came to me late at night, or actually early morning. I woke and had the idea already in my head. I got up and started typing at my computer. I am certain my creator whispered the whole idea into my mind and for that I am grateful. The story came together a few chapters at a time, then there would be a week of nothing. My wife Linda, was very patient as I would be held up in my office for hours. Upon writing this book, I realized I should have paid closer attention in English class.

Thank goodness for editors and google.

To the reader, this is a story of fiction. I know sea life does <u>NOT</u> act like this in nature. This book is about friendship and the need to survive.

We have all been given a gift with this world. Please enjoy the time you have here.

Now, a big thank you to all who helped with completion of my story. Linda and Paulette, my beta readers. Ethan for his illustrations, Eric for the book cover art concept. Marisa, my editor. Mark Phillips for publishing assistance. Various friends who I borrowed some names from. WORD for correcting my spelling as I wrote. And of course, Okent for sharing his story so I could put it on paper.

Donate To Help Okent's Extended Family

Please do your own research if you wish to donate to a charities for orcas, dolphins or whales.
I have included these two charities contact information.
ORCACONSERVANCY.ORG
CONTACT@WHALES.ORG
I recommend the documentary BLACK FISH

ABOUT THE AUTHOR

I grew up in Massachusetts and my family would vacation on Cape Cod. I realized how much I enjoyed the beach, the ocean creatures and life by the sea. My favorite books and magazines would be about the ocean and its many, many creatures. I moved to New Hampshire in 1995. I started a small but successful interior/exterior painting business, which I still operate. I live in a little town in New Hampshire. I share my house with my wife Linda. We are visited throughout the year by deer, owls, foxes, ducks, hummingbirds, fisher cats, bobcats, bears and mosquitos. Interests include biking, hiking, traveling and playing bass guitar in rock bands.
My newest interest, writing books.
Look for WHITE FIN
Unknown Sea

Loutt's Statue in Portsmouth NH

Babel & Baby Okent